Over
The Garden
Fence

Patsy Collins

To my dad – Clive Collins

You taught me how to grow a lot
of things… including stories.

Contents

1 Black And White

Black

The last time I saw my cousin, Felicity, was just weeks before her death. She'd moved to the countryside and invited me to stay. Actually she'd lived there for months and invited me repeatedly, but I'd been too busy. She'd asked me again by phone and something in her voice convinced me to accept.

In the train down I puzzled over what could be worrying her. Maybe the locals didn't like newcomers and were giving her a hard time. Perhaps the cost of maintaining her cottage was more than she'd anticipated and she'd run into financial trouble. She might be ill.

When I saw her waiting on the platform, I was initially reassured. She looked healthy and was dressed in an outfit I'd not seen before. I'm no fashion expert, but I think I'd have remembered that long purple dress with matching button boots and shawl.

"Benjamin! How lovely to see you," she called the moment I stepped off the train. She hugged me.

"You're looking well, Felicity."

She nodded, but her beaming smile didn't make her eyes sparkle the way they usually did.

"If it's all right with you, I thought we'd stop off in the village and pick up a few things."

I readily agreed, assuming it was a long drive from her

cottage to the shops. Certainly her letters suggested going into the village wasn't something she did regularly.

The shopkeepers greeted her by name and seemed very eager to please. Even the children we saw were charming.

"Hello, Mrs Darke," they called, before nodding politely to me and scurrying away. More than one kid offered to carry Felicity's purchases to the car.

It took less than ten minutes to drive back to her cottage. Allowing for parking, I imagined it would be nearly as quick to walk. Why did she make the journey so infrequently and why had she sounded unhappy on the phone? Felicity would explain in her own good time.

Felicity's cottage was stunning, from the straw bird ornament on the thatched roof, right down to the black cat sunning herself in a flower bed. White-framed leaded windows glanced out through roses and jasmine which swarmed over the welcoming porch and scaled the building. Fragrant herbs lined the front path. As I followed my cousin I brushed against these, releasing a strong, medicinal scent.

Felicity showed me to a spacious room.

"I'll leave you to freshen up," she said.

Before I went in search of the bathroom I looked out over her garden. I saw a stone patio surrounded by a profusion of flowers, a grassy area and, right at the back, neat rows of what I guessed must be vegetables and fruit bushes.

Soon I was downstairs again. "I can see why you wanted to move here. You've obviously made the right decision," I said as she poured boiling water into a huge teapot.

"Why do you say that?"

"Well, it's beautiful and you have so much space." Personally I'm happiest in my flat in town, but I knew my cousin felt very differently. "And everyone seems friendly. The children certainly have much better manners than in town." As I continued my praise of her new home it occurred to me I must be telling her things she already knew. I also realised Felicity was barely speaking.

She served me with the most delicious caraway cake and shortbread scented with lavender flowers.

"Gracious, I didn't think it was possible, but your baking has actually improved. These are fantastic."

"Thank you. Now I've got my little bit of garden, I'm able to grow more herbs than I could on my balcony and I've been experimenting."

She offered a delicate sponge flavoured with lemon verbena.

"Wonderful. Treats like this must make you popular with the local kids."

"Not really. They're scared of me. Think I'm a witch."

I nearly laughed, but Felicity's expression showed this wasn't as funny as it sounded. "That's not good."

"No, but at least they leave me alone. There's no vandalism or loutish behaviour."

"I suppose so," I conceded doubtfully.

"I'm lonely though."

I nodded encouragingly. Clearly this was the thing she was unhappy about.

"I wouldn't want them hanging around all the time, but it would be nice to see some friendly young faces occasionally. Say carol singing or trick or treating."

"Surely they'll come for that? Isn't a witch the right person to visit at Hallowe'en?" I suggested, though October was several weeks off.

"Not if you think she's a real one and can do you harm."

"No, I suppose not, but why would they think such things?"

"Apart from me dressing the part and having a black cat?" She stroked Murgatroyd.

I had to admit my cousin's favourite long dresses were a bit witch-like. Her prominent nose and flowing red hair added to the illusion, as would her cackling laugh although it didn't seem likely that had been heard recently.

"And I grow lots of herbs."

"For cooking and because they look so pretty in your cottage garden." I felt I was continuing an argument I'd already lost.

"Ah, but that's full of poisonous plants."

"People say that?"

"It's true. Foxgloves, laburnum, monk's hood."

"They're all normal flowers though, aren't they?" The names sounded familiar and in the brief look I'd had of the garden, I hadn't seen anything sinister-looking.

"Yes and deadly poisonous."

"I can't see why any of this would make people think you're a witch."

"I told them I was."

"Why?"

"I wanted peace. That's why I moved out of the town, but it was the traffic and blaring radios and alarms I wanted to get away from, not decent people."

"Yes, I can understand that, but I still don't follow why they'd believe you're an evil witch capable of doing harm." Having her wild hair trimmed a bit might help her image, I thought, but didn't know how to tactfully suggest such a thing.

"I sort of proved it. The day I moved in, some kids came round watching my furniture being unloaded and generally

4

getting in the way. Not doing any harm I suppose, but I was tired and stressed out and snapped at one of them who'd picked up a flower pot. He dropped it and scarpered when it smashed. He tripped over Murgatroyd as he ran off."

"Oh dear." Annoying Felicity was one thing, hurting her cat wasn't something she'd easily forgive. I wondered where Murgatroyd was; she seemed to have vanished. I shivered. I hadn't realised it, but as we'd been talking dark clouds had formed in the sky, and the day grown cool.

"She screeched at him. I shouted that if he wasn't careful he'd be the one broken and crying. The next day he fell and broke his arm. He remembered me shouting and thought he'd been cursed. I encouraged that."

"I see."

A low rumble of thunder was quickly followed by heavy rain.

"If I heard about someone being ill I'd say that meant they'd drive more slowly past my house and not risk injuring Murgatroyd. When a child fell in the stream, losing his catapult and catching a cold I nodded as though I'd expected it to happen. Soon any misfortune or accident was attributed to me and people wondered what the victim had done to annoy me."

"I'm surprised people are so superstitious, even in the countryside."

Lightning flashed, making me jump. The thunder afterwards came quickly, suggesting the storm was almost overhead.

"Oh, I don't think most people really believe I'm a witch, they just feel a bit uncomfortable around me."

"So, if we can prove you're not a witch, things will improve?"

"Probably but how can I prove that?" She sounded as though she'd given up hope.

"I'll have a think about it."

Unfortunately I didn't get the chance. There was a knock at door. Felicity opened it to reveal a terrified child holding a very bedraggled Murgatroyd.

"Mrs Darke," the girl stammered.

Felicity snatched her cat from the girl and shouted curses. The poor kid sprinted away into the rain. I couldn't think of a way to convince people my cousin wasn't really a witch because in that moment, I too had been sure she was one.

The following morning, I had a call from the office and regretfully told Felicity I'd have to return that very day to my flat in town. That's why I didn't learn about the accident until later. The girl had been so scared she'd not cared where she ran. She'd taken an overgrown footpath as the most direct means of escape and fell, breaking her leg. It took well into the next day for her family to find her. By then she'd lost a lot of blood. For three days they didn't know if she'd live or die. When she regained consciousness she told them of the curses Felicity spat at her.

It wasn't hard to guess what happened next. The uneasiness around Felicity increased and changed into hatred. A week later, her cottage burned down with her inside. I don't know for sure, but I think a human hand, rather than magic or accident, caused it.

White

On the train journey to cousin Felicity's new home I wondered how she was getting on. Was she really as happy as she said, or just putting on a brave face?

When I saw her waiting on the platform, I was reassured. She looked happy, if eccentric, in a long purple dress with matching button boots and shawl.

"Benjamin! How lovely to see you." She hugged me.

"You're looking well, Felicity."

She nodded. Her beaming smile and sparkling eyes were just as I remembered.

"If it's all right with you, I thought we'd stop on the way home and pick up a few things."

I readily agreed. The shopkeepers greeted her by name and were eager to please. Even the children we saw were charming.

"Hello, Felicity," they called. More than one kid offered to carry her purchases to the car. "Can't have a poor old lady like you struggling." They giggled when she waved a fist in mock annoyance and said that for their cheek, they jolly well could do the carrying. Back at the car she produced small cotton pouches for each as a reward.

"Home-made fudge," she told me as she drove home. "I don't think kids should expect to get paid for every little job they do."

Felicity's cottage was gorgeous, from the cooing pigeons on the thatched roof, right down to the silky black cat sunning herself against the warm brick walls. The welcoming porch was almost smothered in dusky apricot roses and creamy jasmine. Honeysuckle twined along the picket fence. Herbs in a variety of soothing greens lined the path. As I followed my cousin, I brushed against these releasing pleasantly sharp scents.

Felicity showed me to a cosy room, complete with antique furniture, chintz bedspread and dark oak beams.

"I'll leave you to freshen up," she said.

Before I went in search of the bathroom I looked out over her garden. I saw a profusion of pastel coloured flowers, a lawn and right at the back, neat rows of what must be vegetables.

Soon I was downstairs again. "I can see why you wanted to live here. You've obviously made the right decision," I said as she poured boiling water into a huge teapot.

"I think so. Shall we have tea outside?"

I assented. "It's beautiful and you have so much space. Everyone seems friendly. The children..." I trailed off as it occurred to me I must be telling her things she already knew.

I helped carry out the tea things. Once in the garden, I saw what I'd thought was a lawn was really a tiny wildflower meadow, buzzing with bees. The lovely flower borders were further decorated with clouds of brilliant butterflies.

Felicity served me with the most delicious rosemary scented scones and rich strawberry shortbread.

"Gracious, I didn't think it was possible, but your baking has actually improved. These are fantastic."

"Thank you. I'm able to grow much more than I could on my balcony and I've been experimenting."

She offered a delicate sponge flavoured with rose petals.

"Wonderful. Treats like this must make you popular with the local kids."

"Well it's either the cakes or the fact they think I'm a witch."

I nearly laughed, but Felicity's expression showed she wasn't joking. "Is that good?"

"Yes. They take care of me and are always running little errands. I never have to go to the shops unless I want to as one of the kids will always go for me."

"Maybe they'd do that anyway, just for the fudge?" I suggested.

"Maybe, but being a witch is fun. I like seeing all those friendly young faces listening to my tall tales of magic spells and love potions. I bet I'll have loads of them round trick or treating."

"Yes, a witch sounds the right person to visit at Hallowe'en," I agreed imagining the kids were making plans though October was several weeks off.

"Especially if they think she's a real one and can grant wishes."

"But why would they think such things?"

"Apart from me dressing the part and having a black cat?" She stroked Murgatroyd.

I had to admit my cousin's clothes were a bit witch-like. Her prominent nose and flowing red hair added to the illusion, as did her cackling laugh. It seemed likely that had been heard a lot recently.

"And I do grow lots of herbs."

"For cooking and because they look so pretty in your cottage garden." I was continuing an argument I'd already lost.

"Ah, but that's full of magical plants."

"People say that?"

"It's true. Witch hazel, heartsease, borage."

"They're all normal plants though, aren't they?" The names sounded familiar and in the brief look I'd had of the garden, I hadn't seen anything sinister. "Anyway, I don't see why growing medicinal herbs makes people think you're a witch."

"I sort of proved it. The day I moved in, some kids came round watching my furniture being unloaded and generally getting in the way. Not doing any harm I suppose, but I was tired and didn't want to deal with them. I told them Murgatroyd was upset by the move and needed quiet. Most went away, but two little girls offered to look after her. They sat out the way, just stroking her gently.

"Good move." Helping Felicity was one thing, being nice to her cat would earn you her undying gratitude. I wondered where Murgatroyd had gone. She followed us into the garden, but then seemed to vanish. I stretched out in the sun, enjoying the gentle, fragrant breeze.

"I didn't have anything to give them, so I said they'd get their reward later. On the way home they found twenty pounds. The owner couldn't be traced so they were allowed to keep the money."

"I see." In the distance, I heard a bird singing a high beautiful tune.

"If I heard about someone getting a promotion I'd nod and say they deserved good fortune because they always drove slowly past my house so as not to risk injuring Murgatroyd. A girl lost the bracelet she was given when she acted as a bridesmaid; I said I hoped it would turn up soon and luckily it was found the next day. When a couple fell in love, I reminded people they'd drunk my herb tea. Soon any good luck was attributed to me and people wondered what the person had done to please me."

"I'm surprised people are so superstitious, even in the countryside."

A small bird flitted over the patio table, making me jump. It flew into a tree and continued its song almost overhead.

"Oh, I don't think most people really believe I'm a witch, they just think it's a good joke and something to gossip about, but plenty think there's no harm being a bit extra nice, just in case."

"So, you like people thinking you're a witch?"

I didn't get an answer. There was a shout from behind the side gate. Felicity opened it to reveal a distraught child holding a bedraggled Murgatroyd.

"Felicity," the girl stammered, "I found her in the pond. I got her out but she wouldn't move."

Felicity scooped the soaking cat from her. The child followed us into the house. Felicity filled a pillowcase with dried herbs to lay Murgatroyd on. She gently rubbed the cat with a cloth, all the while murmuring soothing incantations. After a minute or so Murgatroyd sneezed then shook herself. Felicity placed her, complete with herb bed, where the sun streamed through the window. "I think she'll be OK now."

I understood why people thought my cousin a witch, because during her care for the cat I too had been sure she was one.

Felicity turned her attention to the girl. "Good gracious, look at the state of you!"

The poor child was damp all over and coated from the thighs down with the most disgusting mud.

"You waded right into the pond to save poor Murgatroyd?"

"I couldn't just leave her, could I?"

Felicity sent her to use the shower, giving her clean clothes to put on. Once she was clean and exceedingly oddly dressed, my cousin the witch brewed up a potion for the girl to take. Assured she'd come to no harm, she drove the girl home, leaving me to keep watch on the now sleeping cat.

The following morning, I had a call from the office. I was enjoying my visit too much and told them they'd have to cope without me. I was glad I stayed, because otherwise I might not have heard the rest of the story. The girl's parents had fallen out over some misunderstanding and separated.

She'd been visiting her father and rather than take her right home and face his wife he dropped her off in the village. As she walked the short distance back she'd seen Murgatroyd chase a piece of silver paper which danced in the breeze. The cat followed it right into the pond.

The girl rescued Murgatroyd and took her to Felicity, instead of going home. The mother, annoyed, rang the father and accused him of keeping the girl longer than agreed. Soon both joined together for the search, realising there were things far more important than their silly quarrel. By the time Felicity reunited them with their daughter and said a few careful words they were once again a family and seemed certain to stay that way.

That, as I said, was a few weeks ago. I'm back at Felicity's cottage now. The garden is full of smoke and the house ablaze; with the light given off from the huge bonfire in her garden. The whole village has turned out for her Hallowe'en party.

I don't know if Felicity has cast a spell, or it's just the magic of the countryside and warmth of the friendship I've found here, but in future I know I'll conjure up the time to visit my cousin far more often.

2 Is There Anyone There?

At first, I thought it was a wrong number.

"No, there's no Rebecca here," I answered before hanging up. I was reasonably polite considering I'd been woken late at night by the caller's inefficiency.

A few minutes later, the phone rang again.

"Is that Rebecca?"

"No."

When, it happened the third time, just as I was almost asleep again, I didn't bother to reply. My bedside clock showed it was just after one in the morning. I yanked the phone socket out the wall. If I'd known I wasn't going to get a decent night's sleep I might as well have gone over my report one more time, or even accepted my sister's invitation to dinner.

Fortunately, despite the disturbed night, my presentation went well the next day. I celebrated by sending my assistant Jenny to fetch me a cappuccino to go with my lunch, rather than making instant with the kettle in my office. I'd finished it and my sandwich when the phone rang. I had to answer it myself. Jenny had muttered something about it being a nice day while she'd cleared space on my crowded desk for the cappuccino and I hadn't seen her since. Reminding myself she was entitled to a lunch break, I picked up the receiver.

"Gilbert's and Sons, Beverley speaking, how may I help you?"

"Is Rebecca there?"

"Who is this?" I shouted. "And how do you know where I work?"

"Who am I?" the voice sounded puzzled. "Who am I?"

Then the line went dead. Incredible, not only was someone harassing me, but she'd had the nerve to hang up on me.

"Do you want me?" a tentative voice asked. The frizzy head of Jenny appeared around the door frame. "I thought I heard you call."

"Just a wrong number." At least she hadn't been gone a whole hour, as I've heard some other staff do.

"Oh, right."

Jenny was soon gone, but she left behind a sigh of relief. I made a mental note not to snap at her for a while. Her meek timidity and silly chatter wasted time and was irritating but I knew from experience that few people shared my drive and work ethic.

I concentrated on my spreadsheet. Try as I might, I couldn't shake the idea that perhaps I should know who Rebecca was. When the phone rang, four minutes after the last call, I again picked it up myself.

"I know you're not Rebecca," the voice said after I'd given the standard company greeting.

"Good, so now you can stop phoning me." I disconnected, feeling a touch of satisfaction that this time I'd taken the initiative. It was the same pattern as the previous night, but unlike at home I couldn't unplug the phone.

Again I tapped figures onto the spreadsheet. I had to click 'undo' as I was watching the clock and not what I was doing. Three minutes after the mystery caller admitted knowing they were messing me about, I decided taking a lunch break wasn't such a bad idea. I'd already eaten my sandwich, but a walk in the sunshine might wake me up a bit.

"Just popping out," I told Jenny as I passed her desk. I thought I heard my phone ring as I walked, briskly, down the corridor.

The walk wasn't a total waste of time. I inspected the rose bushes I'd approved the purchase of in my first week with the company. Checking them was somebody else's job, but I knew the best way to get a job done properly was to do it myself. I still couldn't understand the point of providing staff with attractive gardens which would surely only encourage them to spend longer outside and less time actually working, but at least the plants were fulfilling their expected function by providing lush foliage and colourful blooms.

Staff taking late lunches occupied benches amongst the flowers. I passed a girl and boy, saw them stealing looks at each other. As their glances met they hastily looked away, the girl blushing. I heard laughter and the sound of running feet. Glancing back I saw the couple brushing away a shower of rose petals. They too laughed. They were fooling around in what was presumably their own time so there was nothing I could do.

The exercise did me good, I was unusually alert during the afternoon and evening. Determined to ensure my state of efficiency continued, I unplugged my phone before doing a couple of hour's work after supper. I received an e-mail from my sister asking if I was OK. Knowing she was more than capable of coming round in person to disturb me, I plugged in the phone and called her back.

"I'm fine," I informed her before she had a chance to tell me what horrible fate she'd thought I'd succumbed to.

"I rang several times, but there was no reply."

"I unplugged the phone so I could get some work done," I told her, hoping she'd take the hint.

"You work too hard, Beverley. It can't be good for you."

"I'm fine." I moved the receiver away as she started on her favourite theme, telling me to delegate more and try to relax. This was followed by the usual invitation to Sunday lunch. Not wanting to hurt her by saying I didn't want to waste a whole afternoon with her family, I said I'd think about it.

"Brilliant!" she said and wished me good night.

I unplugged the phone again before going to bed. I dreamed a woman called Rebecca told me to stop and smell the flowers.

The following day at work, just before one, the telephone rang. Yet again, Jenny wasn't there and I had to answer it myself.

"I'm Rebecca," the voice informed me. "Learn from my mistake." She disconnected before I could say a word.

Despite the sun streaming in through the window, I felt cold. The sound of a door closing told me Jenny was back from wherever she'd been. Picking up a file at random, I walked through to her desk.

"I haven't been out for long," she stammered. "Just long enough to eat my lunch."

"Right," I agreed. It was true, she'd only been away from her desk for a few minutes. "No problem."

"Is that OK?" she asked, gesturing to the file I'd grabbed.

It was the draft of another report I'd asked her to type up and which I'd not yet had time to double check.

"Yes, fine," I said, returning it to her.

Jenny looked surprised as well she might; I never brought reports back saying they were fine. I always left work in my in tray for her to collect and if it was a first or second draft, I always attached sticky notes suggesting improvements. There was probably something that could be improved in this one too, but as with every other report, probably something so minor, no one but me would even notice much less demand the whole thing be redone.

"Good job," I added.

She beamed at me, though she must have been wondering why I was still there.

"Get that will you?" I said.

"Get what?"

"The phone, can't you hear it ringing?"

"No."

I snatched up the receiver in irritation.

"Ask Jenny about Rebecca," the caller said.

Somebody from the company must be making these calls. Didn't they have any work to do? I stormed out the building. Without realising it, I again walked to the rose garden. I didn't want to, but I bent to sniff a rose.

"Lovely aren't they?" a young woman asked. "I like the deep red ones best." Where the sun shone through her long hair, it glowed the same rich shade as the flowers. "How about you?" she asked.

"The pink," I said spotting some in that colour. It seemed quicker than explaining I didn't have time to waste on such things.

To avoid further discussion, I walked towards the appropriate bushes. The neat flowers were a pleasing shade and the scent was indeed superior to that of the darker roses.

A sleeping pill ensured no ringing phones or incomprehensible dreams disturbed me that night. Nothing at all happened to explain why, at quarter past twelve the next day, I suggested to Jenny that we take our sandwiches into the garden.

She looked surprised, but agreed.

"Do you know about Rebecca?" The words were out before I'd realised I was going to ask.

"Yes. It was so sad."

"Tell me."

"She worked here before you." Jenny seemed unusually reticent.

"Please, I feel I need to know."

"She died. Oh, it was awful. Her heart. Stress, they said it was. "

"She worked hard?"

"Yes, just like you. Oh, I didn't mean..."

"What did she look like?"

"Slim, pretty, long red hair." She glanced at her watch. "Maybe we should get back to the office?"

"Yes, but let's walk the long way round and smell the flowers," I said.

We paused by my favourite pink roses. I checked the name tag – 'Remember Rebecca'.

"Lovely aren't they?" Jenny asked.

"Yes, they are." I made a silent promise to take the time to enjoy them every day.

I didn't unplug the phone that night. Rebecca doesn't need to ring me again and besides I needed it to call my sister and accept her invitation to lunch.

3 Hot And Bothered

Yvonne couldn't decide which dress to wear. What she needed was a second opinion. Right on cue, her phone burst into 'Donald Where's Your Troosers?' indicating her friend Sue was calling.

"Just wanted to remind you, no resolutions this year!"

"Don't you start," Yvonne said. "Why does everyone act like my resolutions are a disaster?"

"Because they are? Last year you said you'd start an evening class and couldn't because it clashed with your boys' swimming lessons."

"I learned with them and the classes were in the evening," Yvonne protested. "So technically that was an evening class."

"Hmm."

"Look, never mind that, what shall I wear tonight? Is my little black number overdoing it for an evening with our neighbour?"

"Don't you mean under doing it?"

Sue had a point. The silky material showed off Yvonne's neat figure and lace panels suggested it revealed even more than it really did.

"The yellow wool one then?"

"Yeah, that's nice. Sensible though. If it's a party, wear the black but don't do anything I wouldn't. Gotta go."

'A bit of a party', was how Yvonne's neighbour Phil had described the evening when he'd invited them. But no, perhaps the yellow wool one would be a better choice.

Yvonne turned her attention to her hair. Should she put it up? After trying different styles she finally pulled it back into a tidy, but boring, ponytail.

Yvonne caught sight of herself in the mirror. Saggy grey bra, mismatched knickers and faded tights weren't a good look. She decided that although the New Year didn't start until the following day she was ready for a new start. She peeled off the offending items pulled on her dressing gown and ran downstairs. Her husband Bruce looked up, but didn't say a word as she chucked her underwear in the bin. Back upstairs Yvonne put on her best set of matching lingerie and a new pair of hold up stockings. That was better. She stood in front of the mirror, stomach held in. The result wasn't too bad.

"Who are you trying to impress?" Bruce asked from the doorway. "Not our new neighbour, the good Dr Matthews?"

"No, silly."

Phil from next door, who'd invited them to his New Year's Eve party, was charming and attractive. He was also ten years younger than Yvonne. At least ten years. She could understand a single woman getting hot under the collar thinking about his bedside manner, but Yvonne didn't indulge in such fantasies. Absolutely not. Almost hardly ever. Anyway she was happily married.

Bruce didn't say he was impressed himself, she noticed. Not that she'd expected it. Lately the only person he seemed impressed with was Tanya, his secretary. She was efficient and friendly, helpful and fun. Yvonne knew this as she'd met the girl, but that didn't stop Bruce reminding her at regular intervals. He never commented on Tanya's looks, but Yvonne was sure her flaming red hair and curvy figure impressed her husband just as much as her typing speeds.

Yvonne took a deep breath. Jealousy wasn't really her style. She preferred to fight fire with fire. She'd remind her husband of her many good points and their happy family life, and make herself as attractive as possible tonight.

Bruce was soon changed into a dark suit and open neck shirt.

"Very nice," she told him.

"Thanks, love. Shall I go and check the children are ready while you finish dressing?"

"Please."

As soon as he left the room, Yvonne returned the yellow dress to the wardrobe and pulled on the black one. She applied extra mascara and added wet-look gloss over her lipstick. She untied her ponytail, leant forward and fluffed up her hair. Then she piled it on top of her head and secured it with glittery clips and pins. Her highest heels, in dazzling pink, completed the look.

She sauntered downstairs and was greeted by gasps from the three kids.

"You're a yummy mummy," Sasha said.

The boys giggled at that, but Bruce didn't seem amused.

Yvonne looked at her children, nicely dressed and on best behaviour so they could attend the party and stay up until past midnight. Surely Bruce must be proud of them and appreciate how lucky he was to be part of such a happy family, even if their mother no longer lit his fire in quite the way she once had.

"Everyone ready?" Bruce asked. As he handed Yvonne her coat he looked at her and seemed to properly notice her for once. He looked her up and down, smiled and said, "Tanya had that hairstyle at the Christmas party. It really suited her."

Yvonne, resisting the urge to let her hair down, clenched

her teeth in what she hoped would pass for a smile. She suddenly wished she hadn't been so quick to throw out her old underwear. There was plenty of wear left in it and it was comfortable, that had to count for something, didn't it?

When they arrived at the adjoining house for the party, Phil was just as complimentary about Yvonne's appearance as the children had been. He kissed her cheek and gave her a hug which he seemed reluctant to end. Yvonne didn't pull away quickly either; her shoes weren't designed for sudden movements.

"He's right, you know," Bruce whispered in her ear, once Phil had let go. "You do look nice."

So, her plan was working! If reminding Bruce of her good points worked, maybe it wouldn't hurt to remind him of Tanya's one bad one. The woman smoked. Hmm, now how could she casually bring that up in conversation? There was one way and she'd be sure to get her husband's attention.

Yvonne bided her time, enjoying the food and conversation with their neighbours until the appropriate moment. At five to midnight, she moved close to Phil, making sure her husband noticed.

"Nearly midnight," she murmured.

"So it is," Phil said. He bent his head to hers and whispered, "There's one tradition I'm particularly looking forward to."

Did he mean kissing as the clock struck? She'd almost forgotten about that. Really she had.

"Any bubbly left in that bottle?" Bruce asked, holding his glass between Yvonne and their neighbour.

"Er, yes. Just opened it," he said and topped up Bruce's glass, then Yvonne's. "So, have you made any resolutions yet?"

"We don't do resolutions," Bruce told him.

Yvonne contradicted him. "Yes, actually I have."

"No!" Bruce half shouted, half sighed. "No more resolutions."

"Oh no, Mum. Please don't," added Sasha. Her brothers joined in these pleas.

"Ignore them," Yvonne said. "They're not impressed with my resolutions, but I'm definitely going to stick to this one."

Bruce looked alarmed. Her children groaned.

"What's so wrong with resolutions?" Phil asked.

"Every resolution she attempts goes horribly wrong." Bruce explained about the year Yvonne decided to lose weight and immediately fell pregnant with their third child, the year she decided to get more exercise and broke her leg and the time she said she'd drink less only to get a mouth ulcer and be unable to eat solids for weeks.

Ignoring this, Yvonne announced, "I'm giving up smoking."

"That seems very sensible to me, Yvonne. Good luck," Phil said.

"But, Mum you don't smoke now," Sasha pointed out.

"Exactly, so nothing can possibly go wrong, can it?"

Despite more groaning from her family, Yvonne smiled confidently. She continued to smile as the clock struck twelve and first Bruce, then Phil claimed a kiss. She positively beamed all through the singing of 'Auld Lang Syne'. Oddly Bruce didn't seem to be having quite as much fun as she was.

The following morning Yvonne and her family hurtled out the house just as Phil walked past with his dog. He didn't ask how her resolution was going; probably the clamour of the smoke alarm and smell of burnt toast had already provided the answer.

A few days later, Yvonne met Sue for coffee. "So tell me the worst. Did you make a resolution?"

"I did. A good one."

"Unlike when you said you'd exercise regularly and then broke your leg in the gym carpark on the second of January?"

"By the time the cast came off I saw how important exercise was. I got myself fit and stayed that way. My other resolutions didn't go entirely wrong either. OK, I did discover I was pregnant with Sasha just after saying I'd lose weight, but I don't regret having my lovely daughter and actually I lost the baby weight, plus a couple of extra pounds by the end of that year."

"Hmm. So what is it this time?"

Yvonne told her.

"I expect fire alarms to sound any minute."

Yvonne explained about the burnt toast.

"Oh dear! But what's with the smoking? You never have."

"Bruce hasn't been taking much notice of me lately and his pretty young secretary smokes. I know he doesn't like the smell and..." she shrugged.

"But Bruce wouldn't..."

"No, I don't think so really. I just felt a bit vulnerable."

When Bruce came home, he said Tanya had already broken her resolution not to smoke. "I'll say this for your resolutions, they might not always go to plan, but you do your best to stick to them."

Yvonne's satisfaction didn't last long. A week later Bruce was praising Tanya's switch to low tar and cutting down to ten a day.

Yvonne's resolution was almost forgotten by the Easter holidays. Bruce took the boys on a bike ride, leaving Sasha to give her mum a makeover. That went well until she decided Yvonne's hairstyle needed attention and scalded her with curling tongs. Yvonne shrieked and Sasha screamed.

Yvonne hugged her near hysterical daughter.

"It's OK, love. It just made me jump, that's all."

"I burnt you, Mum."

"A bit, but it was an accident and I'll be OK."

"But your hair is on fire."

It was true, there was a distinct and very unpleasant smell of burning. There was also the sound of banging at the front door and Phil's voice calling, "Are you all right?"

"I've set fire to Mum," Sasha called. She ran to let him in.

Phil checked the tongs were put safely away, then carefully bathed the scorched skin on Yvonne's neck.

She was very aware of his gentle touch and the glamorous makeup she'd been persuaded to apply.

"Sasha gave me a makeover," she explained.

"And a lovely job she's done too," Phil said.

"Mum's really pretty isn't she?" Sasha prompted.

"Indeed she is." His fingers lingered on Yvonne's shoulder as he pressed cooling damp cotton against her skin. "Would you like to come round to mine for a glass of wine to help with the shock?"

Reluctantly she declined. Even with Sasha as a chaperone, it didn't seem a good idea.

Yvonne didn't have to worry whether to tell Bruce; Sasha gave him the whole story the moment he and the boys returned. The children then disappeared to watch a film.

"So, Dr Phil thinks my wife is pretty, does he?"

"Apparently," Yvonne said. She was a little miffed Bruce seemed surprised. "And my neck's fine now. Thanks for asking." She almost regretted not finding out just how good the doctor could make her feel.

"I've been thinking about the barbecue," she said.

"Really?"

They always held their first barbecue of the year at the end of the Easter holiday and this year's promised to be the best ever. Phil wanted to become involved and they'd already taken down a couple of fence panels between the gardens to make more space. They'd invited everyone in the street, the children's friends and their families, plus a few extras. Surely Bruce wasn't going to show his jealousy by suggesting they cancel?

"Given your New Year resolution, maybe we should avoid flames and have a garden party instead?"

"Actually, Phil suggested the same thing."

"Sensible man. Oh and I thought I might ask Tanya along."

"Lovely," Yvonne said through gritted teeth. She'd invited a couple of work friends so couldn't really object to him doing the same thing.

Yvonne decided Sasha might still be upset over the hair incident, so suggested they go to the salon together before the garden party. "We'll both have our hair done and I'll get made up too. As you did a great job of my makeover, I'd like you to pick the styles and colours and everything."

"Brilliant, Mum. You should have a new dress too."

Could Yvonne help it if Sasha's idea of a good look was a slinky red dress, matching nails and lipstick, towering heels and flirty curls? It would have undermined her confidence to wear anything else. Yes, most definitely it would.

Yvonne looked good, she knew she did even before Bruce gave a low whistle and said his two girls were beautiful. When Tanya arrived he complimented her appearance too, but Yvonne was sure the warmth in his tone was little more than polite.

Sue agreed with her. She seemed to share Yvonne's opinion of Phil too. "I wouldn't mind taking a dose of his medicine!"

Phil greeted Yvonne with a kiss and a hug, even though he'd spent the morning with her preparing the food. "Yvonne, your resolution has completely failed. You look absolutely smokin', babe!"

"Yes she does – and she's all mine!" Bruce said. He put his arm around Yvonne with a possessive air. He pulled her close and whispered, "You're smoking and I'm on fire." Then almost as an afterthought he said, "Phil, I'd like to introduce you to Tanya, I think you two will get on very well."

Bruce led Yvonne into a quiet corner. He kissed his wife then asked, "So, what do you think of my matchmaking attempt?"

Yvonne looked over to where they had their heads together, looking at the selection of music CDs. "They make a good-looking couple."

"Not nearly as good as you, my love."

The stereo burst into life with 'Firestarter'.

"Come on," Yvonne said. "They're playing my song."

4 Unexpected Valentine

Every year just before Valentine's Day, I selected a card and gift for the man I loved.

"Thanks, Maria," he'd say and kiss me.

Not any more. No more Valentine's for me. I don't want to see signs advertising gifts and romantic breaks. I don't want to see the people buying cards, wearing secret smiles or guilty looks. I don't want to see couples; not happy ones or those whose love, like mine, is gone.

I don't hope for a pink envelope through the letter box. I don't hope for the bell to ring heralding the arrival of a scented bouquet or luxury chocolates. I most definitely do not want to see any red roses. February 14th is just another bleak winter's day.

It hasn't always been like that. As a teenager I bought the sentimental cards and sent them to boys. I eagerly raced my sister to scoop up the post.

"I've got four, you've only got two," I'd gloat.

"But, Maria, mine are bigger, and look this one's padded."

"And I bet I get more chocolates too," I responded.

Then I'd met Nigel so I only needed to buy a single, thoughtfully chosen, expression of my love. Only hoped to receive the one card. He never forgot. Often there would be a red rose or Belgian truffles too. I was happy. Nigel worked away a lot, time with him was precious, not a single moment was wasted. I would have liked an engagement ring, he bought me a watch.

"So you can count the minutes 'til I'm here."

"I wonder if our children will have my curly hair, or your freckles," I asked one day. Nigel changed the subject.

I knew his career was important, that he wanted to concentrate on that first, building a secure future for us. I tried not to be impatient.

I was selecting my fifth valentine to him when he passed the shop carrying red roses. Lots of them. I called his name and rushed out, eager for a hug. He was gone. Of course he was. He didn't want to spoil the surprise. I was able to look convincingly surprised when he did present me with flowers. It was easy. He gave me a spectacular spray of freesias, orchids and carnations, all in palest pink. I didn't understand, but said nothing. We had only an hour before his business trip.

I saw him next as I was leaving a train and he boarded another.

"Nigel, you're going on another trip? Give me a call about Saturday."

He just waved.

"Do you know my husband?" a small, thin woman asked.

"Don't think so. Sorry I don't know you, do I?"

"Nigel, my husband just got on that train."

"So did Nigel my boyfriend. What a coincidence."

"Nigel Welland?"

"No coincidence."

"We'd better talk."

She did talk, to me and then to her solicitor. After his divorce, Nigel and I married. His first marriage had been a mistake. His wife was not kind to him. I could well believe him, she hadn't been all that nice to me either.

Sophie, Nigel's daughter, often stayed with us. At thirteen, she acted as her mother's bridesmaid before coming to live with us. By the time she was sixteen her father started buying more flowers that weren't for me. It was Sophie who explained, gently, that history appeared to be repeating. It was not on Valentine's Day that Nigel left, but soon after. On Valentine's Day the following year, our divorce was finalised.

Cards and flowers still came to the house each year, but they were all for Sophie. First there were lots of cards and then just one each year. She married James, the boy who sent it. I was glad she was happy but missed her so much. They visited often, more so after her mother moved abroad and her father began cheating on his third wife.

"We'll always be family won't we, Maria, whatever the rest of them get up to?"

"Of course we will, love."

Sophie worried about me being alone and tried to persuade me to join a club in the hope of meeting someone new. I told her that I was fine without another broken heart. She never stopped trying.

"There's a singles dance the Friday after next, why don't you go? You're a good dancer."

"I would like to go dancing, would you come with me?"

"You're kidding. I can't pass as single, there is so obviously more than one of me." She patted her stretched maternity dress.

"Did you say single?" I asked checking the calendar. "Valentine's Day? You want me to go out, alone on Valentine's Day. No, I won't."

"Sorry, please don't get upset. I just want you to have a bit of fun."

"Like your father does?"

Sophie left then. I didn't blame her. It was a cruel thing to say, she wanted me to be happy and I'd hurt her. We didn't stay annoyed with each other for long. The following week I took her to hospital for a routine check.

"Everything is fine, but I hope your bag is packed. I think this one's impatient to see the world," said the midwife performing the scan. "I'll print this out. Would granny like a picture too?"

Granny did.

Today is Valentine's Day. I see the postman at the top of the road, there'll be nothing for me but I don't care. I find a silver frame for the ultrasound image of my grandchild. I don't need, or want, anything else. The postman goes by. Good. A van pulls up outside, a girl gets out, bringing a box of orchids. She delivers them next door. Good. There is no delivery today that could possibly interest me.

My mobile rings.

"Maria, come quickly. Please I need you."

"Sophie?"

"You are coming?"

"I'm on my way. Stop talking and start breathing."

Sophie gives birth to my grandson whilst holding my hand.

Every year just before Valentine's Day, I select a card and gift for the man I love. "Thanks, Granny," he says and kisses me.

5 Lucky Break

Caitlin crossed her fingers and checked her reflection in the hallway mirror. Did the dressing on her forehead show? If she could hide it under her fringe, she could say she was late because she'd been visiting Derek's mother. A visit to the surgery wouldn't be so easy to explain.

"What are you doing out there?" Derek called, from the lounge.

"Nothing." She turned guiltily away from the mirror, knocking it as she did so. It crashed to the floor.

Caitlin screamed as glass scattered everywhere. Derek came running.

"It's all right, Caitlin," he said, hugging her. "Come on, come and sit down." He took her into the lounge and settled her on the sofa.

"It's just glass, it doesn't matter. Are you hurt?"

"No."

Derek checked her hands for cuts. There were none. Fortunately, she was wearing trousers; bare legs wouldn't have escaped injury.

"I'll make you some tea, then I'll sweep up and everything will be fine."

Caitlin knew nothing would be fine. It was her own fault too, it was silly to worry about Derek seeing the cut, he might have teased her, but he would have been sympathetic. Now she had something serious to worry about. Seven years bad luck, that's what a broken mirror meant. She began to cry. She'd just ruined their future.

The last few years with Derek had been wonderful. She'd been so lucky to meet him. They had literally bumped into each other, she'd been so busy looking at the cracks in the pavement that she hadn't noticed him.

He had laughed when he heard about her superstitions. "You'll get on well with my mum," he said.

He was right. Caitlin knew Derek's mother had bought a lovely topaz necklace so there would be something blue for the wedding. She had searched the loft for her own veil to provide something for Caitlin to borrow. So far, Derek hadn't proposed, but his mum said she knew he would. Caitlin wasn't concerned about an extravagant ceremony; she just wanted to know that Derek loved her enough to make her his wife. That would give her the emotional security she longed for. She'd been sure he'd ask her on their last anniversary, but she'd ruined that hope. He had given her a present. Caitlin had placed it on the coffee table before kissing him. The gift was a pair of beautiful new shoes. Realising she'd brought bad luck on them she'd been unhappy all evening and not surprised when Derek hadn't proposed.

Derek brought in tea and tissues. He gently wiped the tears from Caitlin's face and noticed the plaster.

"Hey, what's this?"

"I banged my head."

"Oh dear, you're not having a good day, are you."

"I think my seven years bad luck started a few hours early."

"What happened?"

"I was making lunch and spilt some salt."

"Which is unlucky?"

"Yes, unless you quickly throw it over your shoulder. I bent down to pick it up and hit my head. I went straight down the surgery to get it patched up. I was nearly home when a black cat crossed my path, so I had to go to your mum's house."

"I don't understand."

"Well, black cats are good luck if you're going on a journey, but bad luck if you're going home. I thought that if I didn't go home, but started another journey, to your mum's, then it would be OK."

"You don't half make things difficult for yourself, don't you?"

"Are you laughing at me?"

"Not really. And not at all when you're hurt and upset. I'll have to find a way of convincing you these superstitions don't mean anything."

"I don't see how."

"Neither do I, yet. I'll talk to Mum."

"But she's…"

"Just as bad? You're right, but I think she'll help."

Caitlin tried not to think about the mirror, or anything else unlucky. At the end of the week, she could no longer stay calm. On Friday the thirteenth a woman who recently broke a mirror is, she felt, entitled to a few nerves. Fortunately she'd already booked the day off work, as had Derek.

"I've got some things to do this morning," Derek said. "Shall I drop you off at Mum's for a while? You can scare each other silly for an hour. When I come back I'll convince you how daft you've both been."

"OK." Caitlin agreed. Derek's mother would be sympathetic.

The women sat drinking tea and wondering about Derek's plan. He was soon back. They heard him clattering around at the side of the house.

"Hello," he called. "I've just seen your neighbours' black cat, is that good or bad?"

"Don't tease us, Derek."

"Sorry, Mum, just joking. Now come into the kitchen."

They saw a box from the shoe shop on the table. Derek sprinkled it with salt, then fetched his mum's umbrella and opened it. His mum and Caitlin just stared at him.

He took Caitlin's hand. "We'll be back in a minute, Mum."

Derek led Caitlin around the side of the house. He walked under a ladder that he'd positioned to block the path.

"Trust me, Caitlin. I want you to close your eyes and take two steps toward me."

"You want me to walk under a ladder?"

"Aren't you already having bad luck because of the mirror? This can't make it worse surely?"

"I don't know."

"Please, try it for me."

Caitlin closed her eyes and took two steps, not even sure if she was stepping on the cracks. She opened her eyes, to see that Derek was down on one knee.

"Caitlin, my love, will you do me the honour of becoming my wife?"

"Oh, Derek! Yes. Yes I will."

They kissed until his mother came out to see if everything was all right.

"Perfect," Caitlin said.

Derek told his mother the good news, then ushered them

both back inside where he opened the bottle of champagne he'd put in the fridge.

"So what's the toast?" he asked.

"Good luck?" his mother suggested.

"Haven't I just proved there's no such thing?"

"No love, you haven't," Caitlin said, removing her locket. "Look what I found whilst you were out."

"A lifetime's good luck, guaranteed," his mum said, sipping her drink.

Caitlin opened the locket, to reveal a four leaf clover.

6 A Misunderstanding

"Ah, here he is, the man I have to thank for twenty-one years happiness," Sue said. She greeted Kevin with a kiss.

It was Sue and David's twenty-first wedding anniversary and they'd arranged a small party.

"Oh yes?" David said. "Is there something I should know?"

"Eh?" Kevin asked.

Sue smiled at their teasing and looked round to check her guests were enjoying the party. On offer was the same food as had been available for the buffet at their wedding reception and the room was decorated with white carnations. Sue had, at David's request, carried a bouquet of those flowers when she walked down the aisle.

All the friends and family who'd attended the wedding had been invited. Most had risen to the challenge of wearing clothes as much like the ones they'd had for the big day as possible. Even a cousin who'd been a baby at the time had got into the spirit and dressed himself in a huge romper suit with a teddy and rattle as accessories. Kevin, Sue's old college friend was wearing an outfit that hadn't even been fashionable in the nineties.

David wore the suit he'd married her in and Sue had her wedding dress on. Luckily her best friend was a seamstress so no one else ever need know the dress had been let out just a little so she could squeeze into it.

People clustered around the happy couple as though they were waiting for something to happen.

"Come on, Sue. I think you'd better explain to your poor husband what you meant about me being responsible for your happiness," Kevin said.

"You introduced us. Surely you haven't forgotten?"

"I did introduce you to a few blokes, I remember that. All of them no-hopers as I seem to remember," Kevin admitted.

"Yes, those that turned up!" Sue said.

"Gawd yes. I was rubbish at matchmaking wasn't I? That's why I gave it up after your last blind date failed to arrive. When I found out he'd chickened out and left you waiting alone in the Frog and Bucket for the third time in a month, I swore I'd never do it again. Thought you'd never talk to me again but luckily you met David about then and were so loved up you'd have forgiven anyone anything."

"No, he did turn up, it was David."

Someone filled Kevin's glass and encouraged him to continue.

"Oh! I get it now," he said. "David saw you that night and chatted you up. I always wondered how you two met."

"It wasn't quite like that," David said, grinning.

"Not at all like that," Sue insisted.

"You chatted me up," David said.

The heads of their guests were going to and fro as though they were watching a tennis match.

"Well you wouldn't talk! I admit that at first I thought you were another of Kevin's no-hopers."

That caused a few giggles, most of which were politely stifled.

"When did you realise I wasn't?" David asked.

"Just now. Well, I pretty soon decided there was some hope for you, but until today, I thought you were the man Kevin had set me up with. I walked into the Frog and Bucket and there you were, alone at the bar and wearing a white carnation. Naturally I thought you were my date and started talking to you."

Friends nodded understandingly.

David grinned. "Ah, that explains it. You're not the sort to walk up to strange men and demand they buy you a drink. I always thought it was my irresistible good looks and magnetic personality, but didn't like to ask in case it wasn't."

That caused a few more giggles, this time less effort was made to keep them quiet.

"David, I came up and spoke to you because you were Kevin's friend, and yes I admit because of your irresistible magnetism."

"But how did you know I was Kevin's friend?"

"Because he'd arranged for us to meet..." she trailed off as she remembered that both men had said this wasn't the case. "But you were wearing a white carnation."

"True," David agreed.

"Why, if it wasn't so I'd recognise you?"

"Because it was my granddad's birthday and he'd been a cut flower grower. White carnations were his favourite, he said they were lucky." David kissed his wife. "Looks like he was right."

7 Children Of The Blue Flower

The food and water are all gone now. It is time to leave my hiding place. I am alive. After what has happened, I am alive. That's all I know, I don't know the time or the day or the month. I think it must be February. I know the year, 2037. That's two things I know, I must learn more.

As I climb the steep steps of the cellar stairs and return to the house, I am surprised by the warmth. It's warmer than spring, as warm as August. No nuclear winter then. Perhaps the heating is on, perhaps it still works. I had not expected power. There can be no power. I am right. The lights don't work. I check the fuse. It's fine, but there's no power. The warmth is coming from outside.

The air is dry and silent and dusty. The wind moves the dust. There is a moisture-free smog of dust hanging; constantly moved into new patterns by the strong wind. I'd call the wind howling, were it not silent. The swirls of dust remind me of the clouds of locusts that were shown on the news.

"A plague will come. Mankind will destroy the plague and himself," the Leader had warned.

The locusts ate through Africa and the Americas and on into the warmer parts of Europe. Then we heard no more. They didn't stop, not then, but the news was all of another disaster. The power plants were no longer within The Company's control. The reactors were now beyond supercritical. There was no way of cooling them. They would

40

melt, radiation would leak then they, and we, would be no more. The only safety would be underground. Details of how to find a place in the shelters would follow. No one cared about locusts after that. Very few stopped to wonder how the shelters had been built, or when, or why.

I look to the horizon. The dancing lights have gone now. The eruptions of orange and pink that lit the sky are there no more. The beautiful deadly sign has faded, ended, gone. I look up. The sky is a mottled, muddied blue. The sun a huge circle of lime green. I am sick; vomit splashes my feet. The sun cannot be green, I won't look up again. The sun cannot be green.

I look at the garden. That too is wrong. The snowdrops had not been showing through the cold earth when my family left, when I shut myself alone into the cellar and pulled the protective shielding over the door. The snowdrops are in flower now. So yes, it's February. I try not to notice the nodding bells are cornflower blue. The leaves that last year were barely glaucous are this year a rich, vibrant, turquoise.

I am a Child of the Blue Flower; trained to appreciate the natural world, to care for the creatures and protect the plants. Our Leader had known what was to come. He had warned; few had listened.

"You who are left will be innocent as children. You will see the blue flowers and know I spoke the truth. You will know how to create the future."

I turn to the golden ivy. Once it had lightened the gloom with a cheerful sunshine yellow, it still echoes the sun's colour. The colour it cannot be. The holly, once smart with a frosting of white variegation, is now neatly outlined in powder blue. I return to the safety of the house. I don't want to see any more.

There is food in the house. There are plenty of tins and

bottles and jars. There are bags of rice and pasta. In the cool of the garage, there are potatoes, carrots, onions, apples and oranges. My mother had sworn I'd be dead by now. She has left me a supply of food. I won't look at the green sun. Mother would not think of me not needing the food.

I try the tap, water flows. It looks clean, safe. Will it be all right to drink, or contaminated? No more contaminated than the air I suppose. I breathe the air; I can drink the water. There is camping gas and a burner in the garage. Five cylinders of gas. Dad said I was a fool to stay. No one could live when the power plants failed. No one could live, yet he bought me spare gas.

I am alive; I know what I must do. I must fulfil the promises we Children made. My task is to follow our Leader's teachings, to meet with the others, to begin again. I see the leaflets stacked for distribution. We were too late, much too late. Less than a tenth were ever delivered, and how many read?

I look at the blue flower that had been our emblem, our sign. I recall the words I helped write. They warn of this, the collapse of the power stations, the changing of the world. Some of the members had been alarmed long ago. The world's power being supplied by one company, The Company, had scared many. Most had been worried about possible high prices, not the end of the world. The Leader, our great teacher had known.

I'd been introduced as one of The Children by Danny. I had tried to persuade my family to listen to the prophecies. They called us a foolish cult and banned me from meeting him. What do I have now? I am a child indeed. I must follow the teachings of The Leader.

The government told us the electricity stations were safe and they built the bunkers. Great underground concrete caves had been prepared. They had known, as The Leader did, of the disaster. They hadn't wanted to prevent it. They'd wanted to survive it. Wanted to triumph. Now no single company provides the power. The government has its own ways of supplying it, deep in the earth. They control the supply, they are the power now. The only power.

"Man will shut himself away from the light and the truth. He will be in darkness for one hundred years," The Leader had foretold.

Whole cities are now entombed together. My family too. The Leader had known the future. He had tried to explain. Those few who listened believed. We became as his children. The Children of the Blue Flower. He could not prevent the power plants imploding, but he warned of the imprisonment of man. He warned of the changes to our world. His children did not want to be buried alive for four generations. We wanted to live on the surface, to breathe fresh air, to see the sun or to die.

Why had he not told me the sun would be green?

I must find the prophecies; then I will know all of the truth. Danny has the scripts. He had allowed me to read some of them when I was with him. Perhaps he would have allowed me to continue after we were parted. I had not asked. I will go to him now and ask. Things are different now.

I pack food into a rucksack and take my brother's bicycle from the garage. It will take an hour to ride through the city, to Danny's house. It will take an hour if I pedal hard, if there are still seconds and minutes and hours.

I find Danny's house. He is not here, but I see that he was. On the table is a vase of flowers. Blue flowers, of course. I remember the argument in our sect about our sign. Some said the flowers should be blue, should always be blue. Others said they should be as far from blue as possible. As the

43

colours returned, we should select the darkest and the lightest to mark the change. I can't remember which was Danny's choice. I look at the flowers. There is no way to tell. They are blue. I haven't left flowers at home. I should have done so. I will leave some here, when I have found the scripts.

In Danny's bedroom, I find photocopied piles of prophecies. 'For the Children' a note says. I take a copy and pack it into my bag. I look in the kitchen, there is no food. I leave what I have brought with me. I pick more flowers and leave the vase next to those that Danny picked. I go home.

I read the prophecies and begin to understand.

"Man's greed and inhumanity will be his destruction and his salvation. The sky will fall in. The poison will be driven away."

The ozone had contracted with the implosion of the power plants. The blue of the distant atmosphere had descended. The pollution had been dragged by the escaping radiation away and above. The sun is still golden. I am viewing it through layers of dust and ozone and pollution.

The sun is not green.

I feel well and strong because the oxygen is now concentrated in a layer close to the earth's crust. The earth has altered in its orbit now. The warmth is proof that the equator, and so the seasons, have shifted.

"Changes will come. The north will move south. A silent wind will warm the land."

The Leader had known so much. He had known that mankind would almost destroy itself. He knew that governments would declare there was no safety. They had taken people below to teach them how to live together. They were beginning again so that when their great grandchildren emerged into the light they would inherit peace. They would live in a simpler world, that they would treasure and protect, not destroy. The Leader had begun to teach us. He wanted us to think for ourselves, to do what we should because it was right, not because it was all we now knew.

"You must learn the way of love and peace. I will teach and you must learn."

The Leader and The Children of the Blue Flower could not teach the people. We could not be heard above the rumours, the fear. When the dancing lights lit up the sky, our families had gone underground. The Children made promises to the people. We shall seek out and care for any who were left behind. We will release pets. We will protect homes. The earth will not wither and die. It will become clean and safe. The great grandchildren of those below ground shall emerge and share the new earth with the descendants of The Children of the Blue Flower.

I begin my tasks. I cycle through the warm wind from house to house. I carry food on my back in case I meet those in need. I do not meet anyone. In each house I tidy and clean. I eat what food I need, take more for my journey. That is all I take. I find no creatures to care for. There are no animals and no birds either wild or domestic. I find only empty cages and empty fields and woods. There are some fish in tanks. I take these to streams and release them. I don't know if they will live. I hear no sounds save the clicking of the spokes on my wheels and the running of water. There are no birds to sing. There are few leaves on the trees. Those few there are, do not rustle in the warm breeze. There are no locusts. There are no people, no voices.

"You will be alone, but you are my Children."

At each house, I find a vase or glass and fill it with water. I pick flowers, the bluest I can find, and I set them where a visitor would be sure to see them. The flowers begin to change. I leave chartreuse daffodils, then navy tulips. Summer brings the blue roses. Once so sought after, now the only option. The spires of delphiniums at least look right. They are the brightest, richest blue I have ever seen.

Autumn brings with it dahlias and chrysanthemums; do I imagine the blue is a little less true? They seem muddier, as though another colour tries to break through. The winter comes, there are few flowers, but more in this warmth than there would have been in previous years. I pick snowdrops again. Maybe they are a little paler now. Maybe I just want them to be.

For more than a year I have travelled. Occasionally I find a vase of decaying flowers and know that I am not entirely alone. Once in the summer the flowers were barely wilted. I thought I might meet Danny. Still I am alone. I am tired. I'm going home.

I enter the house and see the vase I had left. The same vase; but not the same flowers. These are still fresh. I look closer. There are primroses of palest moss green, there are hellebores, with the faintest rim of muddy maroon. There are tulips, just showing colour. Colour that is not green. I look closer still and see drops of dew still clinging to the newly picked buds.

I listen, and hear Danny call my name.

8 Extra Gran

"I'm sorry love, I know you're upset, but we need to talk." Darren took my hand, leading me away from the room in which the old lady lay dead. "We have to decide what we're going to say," he continued.

"We'll tell the children the truth; they're old enough to understand."

"Of course they are; I didn't mean them."

"Who then?"

"The authorities."

"What authorities? What are you talking about?"

"We'll have to get a death certificate, have her buried."

"Yes, obviously."

"They'll need to know who she is. Was, I suppose I mean."

"But, we do."

"Sorry, Joanne, but we don't really."

He was right of course, I knew that, I'd simply forgotten. Funny really, the things you can forget.

I remember the day I first met her. I'd just discovered I was pregnant and raced to tell Darren. I'd burst into his office without thinking. He'd hugged me and laughed. I didn't realise he wasn't alone until after I'd told him our good news.

"Congratulations, my dears," his visitor had said.

"Oh Lydia, I'm so sorry," Darren stammered.

"Oh don't worry about me, it does me good to see people happy," she'd answered.

She'd gone on to wish us joy of our growing family. Her words were so obviously genuine they really moved me. I knew that if she was seeing Darren professionally then she had her own problems.

Darren never normally discusses his cases. He wouldn't have mentioned Lydia again if I hadn't asked. Maybe because I'd met her it seemed different.

"Doesn't she get on with her family?" I asked. "That's why she said all that stuff about holding on to each other?"

"She doesn't know who they are."

"Why not?"

He hesitated before telling me, stroking my still flat stomach as he decided what to say. He knew me well enough to know it had to be the whole truth, or nothing.

"It seems she had some sort of accident. She was found; years ago this was, lost in a wood. She was wearing filthy tattered clothing and was very thin and dehydrated. She couldn't remember who she was. The first night she kept calling 'Lydia' in her sleep. When she was questioned in the morning she still couldn't remember anything. When they asked if Lydia meant anything she just said it was a pretty name. That's how she came to be called it. The woods were inspiration for her new surname. Although she recovered quickly, she never regained her memory. She's been searching for a family ever since."

"Lydia was my mum's name."

Darren squeezed my hand. He knew the story as well as I did. My parents had been driving myself and my grandmother to the beach to make the most of an Indian summer when they'd crashed. Aged two, I'd become an orphan. I'd been lucky; I was fostered and adopted by a wonderful couple. They already had five children of their own, but had plenty of love left over for me. I'd benefitted then, and still do, from a caring extended family. I felt so sorry for Lydia who had been alone all those years.

"You said this was years ago; how many years?" I asked Darren.

"Twenty-two."

"What month?"

"Early November."

It was in late October, twenty-two years previously that my parents had died. After a little research, we discovered that the woods in which Lydia had been found were just a few miles from the beach that was nearest the town in which I'd been born. Lydia was not my mother, I knew she had died, not disappeared. The amazing coincidence of us both being robbed of family memories in the same place at the same time formed a bond between us.

By the time our son, John, had been born, Lydia had moved into a flat in the street next to ours. She sat with my adoptive mother as I gave birth. We began to call her 'extra gran'. She was a wonderful great grandmother to the children. She helped look after John whilst I gave birth to Emily and then both of them, when I went in to have Rebecca.

Darren's parents and my adoptive family were supportive too of course, but they already had grandchildren. Their time was divided up amongst several children and their other interests. It was different for Lydia; we were all she had.

She lived in her flat, visiting us often for twenty-three years. Lydia got ill just a few months after Rebecca left home. No one knew her exact age, but she was by then a very old woman. It seemed natural for her to move in. She was very easy to look after for the few weeks she lived with us, not that I'd have begrudged nursing her, had that been necessary.

It turned out that Darren needn't have worried; there was no problem in registering the death. Paperwork had been raised once it was clear that her memory would not quickly return and she was given a new legal identity.

We had her buried next to my parents and grandmother. The headstone reads 'Lydia Forrest, devoted and beloved Extra Gran of John, Emily and Rebecca'.

"I don't know who you were before I met you, Lydia," I whisper as I lay flowers on her grave, "but that's certainly who you were from that moment on."

9 A Garden Visit

Maddie ripped open the padded envelope. There was a CD in there. It would be a recording from her brother. She put it in the machine and pressed play.

'Hi, Sis. Hope all's well with you and you're not too hot. On the news they're talking about bush fires because of the heat, but I don't think they're near you?' Bruce began.

It was funny, they'd thought, he was the one with an Australian sounding name.

"Maybe that's what put it into Dad's head to go over there?" he'd wondered.

They'd never got an answer to that. Dad hadn't done explanations. Still she and Bruce found each other.

That they lived on opposite sides of the planet and hadn't known about each other until Maddie was thirty and Bruce was half as much again, didn't seem to matter at all. Despite all that they'd become very close and corresponded regularly. Or maybe because of it? If teenage Bruce had accompanied his father from England, would he have cared about his new, helpless half-sister? Knowing him now, she imagined he'd have looked out for her.

Thinking of what might have been wasn't something Maddie enjoyed. Instead she listened to her brother's words and was grateful for the relationship they did have.

'Put a coat on, Sis. We're going for another walk round the garden.'

In reality Maddie had never been to England, but in her mind she'd walked round Bruce's garden dozens of times. This would be her first winter visit though.

'Can you smell that? The daphne has just come into flower. That sweet lemony tang almost makes me hungry.'

She nodded in agreement. Apartment dwelling Maddie knew what the shrub smelled like, because she'd asked a friend take her to a plant shop and help her find one in flower.

'Feel this, Sis. That smooth, silky bark is a cherry tree. In spring it'll have the most delicate blossom, in summer there'll be luscious fruit if the birds spare me any and in autumn the leaves will turn an almost glowing pink before they fall. Even without all that I'd grow it, just for the pleasure of running my hand over the trunk.'

Maddie's hand longed to touch it too.

'Bend down close to the heather,' Bruce said. 'Can you hear that bee working it? I thought they hibernated but perhaps this is his version of a midnight feast?'

She really could hear it! He must have put the recorder right up to the creature and it had been so intent on gathering nectar it hadn't taken flight.

'And here's something you might recognise even though this little bush ain't a patch on the trees you have out there. That's it, sniff the resinous scent and feel the leathery leaves. Got it?'

"Eucalyptus!" Maddie said at the same time his recorded voice said the same thing.

Bruce had flown out to see her last year. That first hug had felt so familiar. Maddie was sure she'd have known he was her brother if she'd met him one day by chance.

It had been winter for him then too. The contrast between

his cold, wet home country and the dry heat of hers must have been huge. Naturally he'd wanted to see something of Australia as well as his sister and they'd travelled during his visit. Seeing her homeland through Bruce's eyes had been wonderful. His enthusiasm as he described their surroundings was so infectious.

"You must come to England," he'd said.

"I don't know if I could."

"Scared of flying are you? Just don't look down and you'll be fine." They'd known each other well enough for him to tease her by then.

"It's not so much the flying as the airports and not knowing where to go."

"Just explain when you book and they'll look after you. They're used to helping people who need it. Plenty of people are put onto little buggy things to get about the airport, or wheeled on in chairs."

"I can walk OK, Bruce." As she said it she stumbled on a rock.

"I can see that! Like I said, you'd be fine and I'll pick you up and take care of you once you're in England."

She'd promised to think about it.

Bruce's recorded garden tour took him across his lawn. 'Proper grass that; lush and green and springy under your feet. Not the scraggy stuff you have over there. Nothing like wandering round the lawn barefoot with a glass of gin and tonic in your hand on a summer's evening.'

Maddie smiled. She'd heard before about Englishmen and their lawns. It seemed her brother was a walking cliché.

The tour continued with Bruce describing the delicate crocus buds and blowsy double hellebores. He almost had her convinced she could smell the aromas of the evergreen herbs he grew by the kitchen door. There was a clunking sound as he lifted the lid of his rhubarb forcer. The description of those tender stems cooked under a buttery crumble and served with a glug of thick cream made her suddenly hungry.

'And down here, Sis, are snowdrops. Such delicate things, but so strong. They remind me of you.'

As he described them Maddie imagined the pure white cups dangling on their delicate stems. She almost felt the slightly succulent leaves between her fingers and smelled the faint honey scent.

'Maddie, come over to England. I want to walk you round my garden for real. You can do it, I know you can.'

Later that day, Maddie made a call to the airline. "I want to find out about flights to England. I'd need a bit of help at the airport as I'll be travelling alone and I'm blind."

Then she played Bruce's recording again and imagined walking round the garden for real, her brother's hand in hers.

10 A Different Linda Jones

I bought the rose after work. Is it wrong that I took it home to enjoy its beauty for a while before bringing it here? I told myself it was an unselfish gesture for her; the dead lady who shares my name. The dead lady who might be the person who saved my life.

Maybe I won't feel guilty once I've given it to her. I waited until evening had almost given way to night to leave my pathetic gift and mumble inadequate thanks unobserved. That was the plan. There's a man kneeling by her grave. I slip into the shadows to wait.

I've been waiting for years, a few more minutes don't matter. I was a teenager when some weird trick of fate blew a loose sheet of the local paper into my face as I'd been walking to the chip shop. I glimpsed my own name. Supper temporarily forgotten, I found a bench and read. The article explained my namesake had been successfully treated for cervical cancer and urged readers to have regular smear tests. "If I'd done that, I wouldn't have needed surgery and chemotherapy," Linda Jones informed me.

Since leaving the children's home I hadn't bothered registering with a GP. My unknown genes kept me healthy; the only gift from my parents and even that hurt. The article stated the other Linda hadn't noticed any symptoms until her condition was far advanced and painful. I registered with a doctor and had the test.

"We've caught it early," my doctor assured me. "I've made

you an appointment at the hospital. We'll soon have this sorted out." He talked me through the simple procedure. "Do you have any questions?"

"Could this be hereditary?"

I learned there was a greater than average chance that my mother had developed the disease. My genes weren't so perfect. Maybe I wasn't abandoned by two healthy adults who simply didn't want me. Perhaps my mother's cancer had been discovered as I was born and she'd been too ill to care for me. It was plausible enough to comfort me a little.

Although I thought of writing to the paper, to say that article achieved its aim, I never got around to it. I should have. My life wasn't so full I didn't have time. It wasn't full at all. Hardly worth saving.

I've worked hard since. Back when I first learned about the other Linda Jones I'd only just scraped enough together to afford a portion of fish and chips. Now I could buy that every night if I wanted, even eat in a restaurant now and then. I was saving for a car and bought a copy of the local paper.

I hadn't read the obituaries of course, but as I folded the paper, ready for the recycling bin, I spotted my own name again. I couldn't be sure it was the same woman, but it's not a big town so it seemed likely.

Attending the funeral didn't feel right, but I wanted to do something. If anyone deserved a gesture from me wasn't it her, the woman who'd possibly saved my life? It certainly wasn't the woman who'd given me life and left me to cope with it alone. I'd tried to find her. I'd filled in all the forms, written letters but I'd not had a single response. So I bought the rose on the way home from work and waited in the dark to leave it.

Waited for the man, her son I guessed, to go. I heard him sob, quietly but unmistakably. Inexplicably I felt a tear slide down my own cheek. He must have loved her to be crying by her grave. She must have loved him. I was sure she did.

Should I approach? Would it comfort him to know I lived and was healthy, thanks to her? Or would it hurt to be reminded of nearly losing her before and realise afresh that this time there'd be no wonderful recovery. As I waited I played out conversations in my head.

He'd be comforted, I decided. As I was never going to speak I could imagine any response I liked, couldn't I? He'd thank me for telling him and say he was pleased that although he'd lost his mother it was good to know her wish to save others had been granted. That would be nice, but then he'd ask about me, wouldn't he? He'd want to know what I'd done with the life she'd given me. I'd have to answer in the same way I'd have answered my mother had she ever bothered to ask. "Nothing."

I have no family, which isn't my fault. I have no friends, no happiness. All my life I've blamed my parents for that. While it's true they left me without those things I could have made them since. Or at least tried. What I have is a rented flat, a job I do OK and enough money to pay for driving lessons. Where did I plan to go once I'd learned? Who would I visit?

The man adjusted the flowers on the grave, whispered a few words and walked away. I didn't go after him. Instead I waited until I was sure he couldn't look back and see me, then took the place he'd vacated. I placed my rose amongst the other flowers.

"Thank you, Linda," I whispered. "I left it too late to thank you for saving my life, but maybe I've not left it too late to make something of that life. I'm going to try, I promise."

11 The Camera Never Lies

The name 'Luisha Summer' wasn't in bigger letters than the rest of the message, but they were all he really noticed. Was she really coming back into his life?

Richard left the email open on his computer, put up the 'back in 5 mins' sign up, locked the front door of his studio and crossed the road to the bakery. He needed a Belgian bun or a doughnut and time to think.

"On your account?" the baker asked as she slid his sugary snack into a paper bag.

He patted his pockets. "Please." Since he'd discovered that children would sit still for just long enough to have their picture taken if given a cake, and also looked cute while enjoying them, he'd been a regular customer at Kerry's Cakes.

Kerry was a good friend, as well as an understanding supplier when he rushed out during a quiet minute and forgot to bring any money with him, or when he had too many quiet moments and couldn't always pay straight away.

Back in the studio Richard made tea and read the email yet again. Yes, it really was offering him the opportunity to photograph Luisha Summer on Wednesday for a glossy woman's magazine. What was more, they were offering to pay considerably more than he earned in the average month.

Who was he kidding? It was more than he'd earned even in a good month lately and there hadn't been many of those since he'd opened his studio. So few that if he didn't accept the commission he wouldn't be able to pay the rent and he'd be out of work.

Hesitating made no sense. There was no difficulty about doing the actual job. Portraits were his speciality and he'd done quite a few portfolios for aspiring models so knew what was required. His premises were to be used so he didn't need to travel or sort out locations and naturally he didn't have anything else booked that afternoon. That's all they wanted from him, one afternoon. A few hours that could save his business. Just the fee would keep him going for a few months and this job could lead to others for the magazine, or the model. Even if it didn't, local girls would love to be photographed in the same location and by the same photographer as Luisha Summer had used. Once his name appeared as a credit next to her photo, he'd be made.

Before he could change his mind, Richard replied to the email accepting the commission. Then he breathed deeply and allowed himself to think of Luisha. For years he'd been pushing the image of that gorgeous face and figure from his mind. He'd better get used to the thought of her before being confronted again with the reality.

She'd been Lucy Winterbottom when he knew her. And she'd been his girlfriend for a time. Sort of. At school she'd been pretty and popular and never even noticed geeky Richard. He'd noticed her of course. Everyone did. When Richard left school he went straight into a job in a photography studios. He'd just been a trainee, but earned enough to pay his keep, run an old banger and take a girl out. That's when Lucy noticed him. He'd photographed a portfolio for her, after hours at work. His boss allowed him to print the photos and bind them smartly for her, taking only the cost of materials from his wages. Richard couldn't remember Lucy hanging around long enough to thank him, but perhaps his bitterness at being used and dumped clouded his memory.

After that he saved his money to buy camera equipment and spent his spare time learning his craft. Photography became his only passion.

Luisha had been an almost overnight sensation thanks in part, he knew, to Richard's work. Was that behind the offer to photograph her now? Was it her way of thanking him; to help his career as he'd helped hers? Could she perhaps want him back? Or was she laughing at him to show how much above him she'd become? He'd thought he'd done well to start up on his own at only twenty-seven, even if his business was struggling a little, but his success was nothing compared to hers.

He almost regretted accepting the job, but really he'd had no choice. The night before the shoot he barely slept. In the morning he swept, dusted and polished the already spick and span studio. He bought fresh flowers. Luisha loved flowers. He bought cream cakes; she looked far too thin in all the images he'd seen of her. Then he bought fresh fruit and bottled water in case she wanted to stay that way.

Richard tried a few exercises to help him relax, then showered in case that had made him sweaty. Then he waited, and waited.

The car swept up outside his studio only slightly more than an hour late. Richard had forgotten how she'd always kept him waiting. This time though it was the man he assumed was her manager who was driving, so perhaps the fault wasn't hers. Without a word of apology the driver identified himself as the man who'd emailed, shook Richard's hand and then introduced Luisha.

Richard said, "Hello, Lucy. Nice to see you again."

She gave the prettiest little frown, then smiled sweetly. "Lovely."

"It's a long while since I photographed you," he prompted.

"You two know each other?" her manager asked.

"Oh... yes." She didn't sound terribly certain. Or perhaps she was embarrassed?

"We were at school together," Richard said. "Well, shall we get straight to work?"

Luisha immediately brightened. She allowed her manager to help her off with her coat, checked her flawless face and hair and took up position between the lighting rigs. She came alive in front of the camera, easily following his directions and taking up and maintaining the poses he requested. There was no doubt she was good at her job.

In contrast, when Lucy was waiting for her manager to hand her a prop or for Richard to change lenses she looked sort of shadowy. It was as though the camera focussed not just her image but the woman herself. Her frown returned when he deliberately called her Lucy and instructed her in the same phrases he'd used years previously. His camera caught the moment she remembered. It wasn't a pretty picture.

Later, whilst processing the pictures, he was drawn to that unflattering image. It was as though he'd seen through her surface beauty and captured what lay beneath. The real Lucy, not airbrushed Luisha. He could easily sell it to a magazine who'd 'exclusively reveal' her as a fake. He could even manipulate the pictures, give her dark bags under her empty eyes, fatten her neck and accentuate her fine wrinkles. He'd make money, probably more than the fee he'd already earned. He wouldn't get another job photographing a top model, but Luisha had just shown him he was such a forgettable nobody it seemed unlikely he would anyway.

His computer skills would make it easy to doctor the picture; his conscience made it impossible. It wouldn't be fair. She'd wounded his pride a little, but she wasn't really a bad person and she certainly wasn't ugly. Besides it could destroy both their careers and his self-respect.

Richard deleted every photo which showed Luisha looking anything other than her very best and set to work on the images he'd been commissioned to produce. He made the usual slight tweaks, to ensure no shadows appeared under her eyes and to highlight her trademark glowing complexion, but it didn't take much. In fact no more than he did for the close-ups of local brides in their wedding pictures. He knew it was far less than was done for many other professional models, whose photos often had pounds and years taken off.

He looked back at the raw images he'd taken. Luisha was just a very pretty girl he once went out with. He'd nursed a heart that had never really broken because it suited him to work long hours and save his money. Perhaps he'd looked for a hidden meaning behind her coming back because now he was ready to look for someone to share his life?

Richard sent off the finished photographs along with his invoice. The bill was paid promptly then a few days later he got a surprise; an enormous bouquet of flowers and a card.

The note inside read:

'Dear Richard,

Thank you so much for the wonderful pictures you took last week – they're fab! And thank you too for the ones you took all those years ago. I don't remember if I thanked you then, but if I did it wasn't enough.

Those photos not only helped start my career, but also helped me through a difficult period in my life. Supporting my mother through her chemotherapy was hard. The excitement of starting my career helped us both cope. So, thank you!

I want to apologise too for not immediately recognising you. That was just sooo awful of me. I promise it's not because I'd forgotten. We had some good times, didn't we in that old blue car of yours? lol You never once moaned when Mum's illness made me late either.'

Richard stopped reading. He remembered now that her mum had been to hospital for tests. He hadn't realised she'd been so ill though. Hadn't known because he'd never bothered to find out. Had he really thought just a few days ago that she was shallow? Back then he'd only ever looked on the surface so of course he'd seen nothing else.

He read on.

'Seeing you made me realise how much I want to come home, so that's what I'm going to do. I'll be away working a lot though, of course. And talking of work (see what I did there!) I was so impressed with yours that I'd like to use you as my main photographer, that's if you don't mind?'

Mind? This is what he'd been hoping for since he first read that email a fortnight ago. This was his business saved. He almost sagged with relief. The last ten years of hard work and loneliness hadn't been in vain.

'Anyway, think about it and stay in touch, OK?

Hugs and kisses Luisha

The same and thanks from Lucy x x x '

Richard did think about it, not for long but long enough for his face to feel a little stiff from the huge grin stretched across it.

"You OK?"

He looked up to see Kerry the baker looking at him with concern. It was only then he realised he was still standing in the threshold of his studio with a huge bunch of flowers at his feet and an envelope in his hand.

"Yes, I'm fine. Just had some good news in fact, about the business."

"You'll be staying open then?"

He blinked. She was so easy to talk to that he'd hardly noticed pouring out his concerns to her each morning.

"I will, yes. And I think it'll be cream cakes every morning from now on."

"That's good news! Well I'd better get back ready to serve you then."

It wasn't long before he followed her. Just long enough to put down the card, secure the studio and pick up the flowers. He ran ahead of Kerry and thrust the bouquet towards her.

She laughed through a face full of petals. "These are for me?"

"Yes. Well, I didn't actually buy them for you," he confessed. "But I'd like you to have them. And, Kerry, I'd like to take you to dinner if you'll let me."

"To celebrate your good news?"

"I don't mind why you come, just as long as you do."

"Then I accept."

As he ate his cake Richard thought of the distorted image he'd almost made of Luisha. Considering producing that had been just one of the mistakes he'd made over her. He wouldn't make another and he'd try not to repeat them with Kerry.

12 A Change Is As Good As A Rest

George waved goodbye to his wife and her friend Laura. "Have a lovely time," he called. She wouldn't hear him inside Laura's Metro, but George meant what he said. It had been an excellent suggestion of Laura's that the girls spend a week together at her house, leaving her husband Bill and George together at his home.

"Think we'll cope all right?" Bill asked. "Our wives have done everything for us for so long, I'm not sure we'll remember how to fend for ourselves."

"Come off it, mate," George replied. "Before we were married we had our mums cooking and cleaning and all the rest. We've never had to do it. No wonder the girls have got fed up."

"I know. I can't even think what we should eat tonight, let alone work out what ingredients to buy and how to cook it."

Jenny waved goodbye to her husband and his friend Bill. "Look after yourself," she called out though she knew her words couldn't be heard outside Laura's little red car.

"Do you think they'll cope OK without us?" Laura asked.

"They're sensible enough not to starve or burn the house down, I think. I'll have a ton of extra housework to do when I get back, but at least George will have learned how much I do for him."

"I feel a bit guilty; my house isn't the one that's going to get mussed up. How about we go out for a meal tonight, my treat?"

"Oh lovely! I hardly ever eat out. George thinks it's a waste of money."

"Same here, Bill does too."

"Oh Laura, I'm so looking forward to this week. It'll be nice to have someone sharing the work of course, but we'll also have plenty of time to chat and do what we want. Shopping for instance."

"That's what I'm most looking forward to. Bill hardly ever really talks to me as he's always too busy with his paper and when we go shopping he's impatient to get out the store before I've looked at more than one or two things."

"George is as bad and at home he just disappears into his shed except for meal times."

As George and Bill pondered how to avoid going hungry, a couple of teenagers walked by sharing a bag of chips.

"There's a chippy near here, then?" Bill asked.

"Yes. Don't know what it's like, mind. I expect everything is fattening and unhealthy."

"And it'll just be plain old cod and chips, not fancy steamed heritage potatoes and salmon on a bed of wilted watercress with a dill dressing or summat imaginative like that."

The boys visited the local convenience store to buy a few ingredients they reckoned they'd manage to cook during the week. On the way home they bought themselves large portions of cod and chips. They ate every scrap, washed down with mugs of tea, before throwing the wrappers away and settling down to watch two Westerns Bill had brought with him.

Apart from a few shouts of encouragement for the sheriff at tense moments they hardly spoke until they said goodnight.

The girls studied the menus, trying to decide which options would do least damage to their diets.

"Although I don't know why I bother. Nothing I do seems to shift the pounds and George tells me I look fine as I am," Jenny said.

"Well you do! Wish I had your figure."

"You're much slimmer than me."

"I don't think so, but let's not worry about our weight tonight, eh?"

Laura chose steak and kidney pie with mash, followed by apple crumble and custard. Jenny opted for stew and dumplings followed by treacle tart and clotted cream.

"I feel even more guilty now. This is just the sort of food George likes. I don't cook it because it's not very healthy, but I have to admit it tastes good."

"Hmm. Delicious. Wonder if I could get away with a few simple dishes like this at home? I try to give Bill an interesting and varied diet, but maybe I shouldn't neglect the classics occasionally."

When the bill arrived, the women agreed the boys had a point about the price. Either of them could have produced just as good a meal at a fraction of the price.

"Still, there's no washing up to worry about, Jenny."

"True, although George usually does ours. The one thing he does do around the house!"

"Snap! Bill's our chief washer upper since he retired."

The girls switched on the television when they got in, but soon muted the volume so they could chat. It was late by the time they'd set the world to rights, updated each other on their families and made plans for the coming week.

When George came downstairs in the morning, Bill already had the kettle boiling.

"Good timing. You fry the bacon and I'll butter the bread once I've made us a brew."

"Right you are."

After they'd enjoyed the bacon butties and tea, George washed up. Cleaning the frying pan and plates didn't really seem any more work than getting all the bits of muesli off cereal bowls.

"Anything in particular you'd like to do today, Bill?"

"I like to read the paper of a morning."

"We'll stroll down and get one then. Should tell us if there's any cricket on."

"Yes, I noticed Jenny took the magazine with the TV listings. Told her there was one at our place."

"Ah, but she'll have marked ours with what she wants to see."

"I take it you're the same as me and don't get a say?"

"Yep. Although actually when it comes to sport, I prefer to sit out in my shed and listen to the wireless."

"No interruptions?"

"Exactly."

They bought a paper each and tutted over the state of the world until lunchtime. After their hearty breakfast they didn't need much so simply shared a tin of soup and followed it with an apple before going out to the shed to listen to the cricket.

"Maybe I'm being whimsical, but shutting me eyes and listening feels almost like being there."

"I'll try that then, George, but give me a nudge if I start snoring."

Bill didn't snore. When the players stopped for tea he said, "I see what you mean about feeling like you're there. Reminds me of watching games on the green with my dad."

"Television's all very well for showing the action, but being able to see everything and watch again in slow motion reminds me I'm not seeing it for real."

"Think you're right. Shall I make us a cuppa?"

"If you like, or you could share my guilty secret." He produced a bottle.

"What you got there?"

"Orange squash. All sugar, colour and flavouring, but I like it."

"Haven't had that in years!"

The light at the cricket ground stayed good so the game went on until supper time. The boys went down the chippy again.

Jenny lay in bed in Laura's spare room until quite late. It wasn't until she'd washed and dressed she realised she'd been subconsciously waiting for George to bring her a cup of tea. When she went downstairs, Laura was just filling the kettle.

"What would you like for breakfast? I have muesli, low fat yoghurt or grapefruit."

They shared a grapefruit which they carefully prepared to obtain maximum flesh with minimum pith. It still tasted bitter.

"Lots of vitamin C in grapefruit," Laura reminded her. "And something to fight the free radicals too, if I remember correctly."

"Yes and they're so invigorating," Jenny added. Neither of them mentioned the flavour, or the mess.

They spent the morning shoe shopping. It was fun to try on outrageous styles they had no intention of buying without having to listen to complaints of time wasting.

"I'm famished now though, we'd better look for some lunch," Jenny said.

"I thought I'd make us a paella tonight so just a snack should be enough."

The girls had cake and coffee. They shopped for clothes all afternoon, doing their best to ignore rumbling tummies. They made their only purchases, the paella ingredients of squid, shellfish and saffron, just before leaving the shopping mall.

It took Laura ages to peel and chop garlic, scrub muscles and oysters, rinse prawns and grate onions. She fretted over timings so nothing was overdone and scalded her fingers fishing out the crustaceans to allow the rice to cook.

Jenny quite enjoyed the exotic meal although she was so hungry by then she'd probably have eaten a plate of cat food with enthusiasm.

The preparation time was nothing compared with the cleaning up. The garlic press was impossibly fiddly, Jenny skinned her knuckle on the grater and dropped the large pan on her foot. By the time they were ready to sit down and relax, Jenny's favourite TV programme was over and the next one halfway through. She couldn't catch up with what had already happened because of Laura chattering away about the things they'd almost bought that day.

"Do you think the boys are missing us?" she asked in a

commercial break.

"I was wondering the same thing. Let's give them a call to check they're OK."

There was no reply from Jenny's home number so she left a message. George rang back just as they'd settled down with cups of tea to watch the last part of a series they'd both been following. After the boys told their wives they were fine and had just popped out to the chippy everyone assured everyone else they were having a good time. The conversation ended shortly before the credits started to roll on Laura's TV screen.

"Jenny, it's bin day tomorrow, isn't it?"

"Will it be the same day for you as it is for us?" she asked to cover the fact she didn't know which day rubbish was collected from her home.

"I'm pretty sure it's tomorrow, but can't remember if it's time for the recycling one or the other."

They checked to see what the neighbours had put out before manoeuvring the awkward wheeled bin into position.

"Actually, washing up might not strictly be the only thing George does at home."

"Bill does our bin too, but then it is a man's job."

George was just assembling bacon sarnies when Bill came downstairs for breakfast.

"Did you know your cistern isn't filling up right?"

"Thanks for reminding me. I'll sort it out after breakfast. Jenny keeps on at me to look at it, but she always mentions it just when I'm going out to the shed. By the time I've listened to the cricket, or done whatever else I was going out there for, I've always forgotten all about it."

The two men soon fixed the plumbing and then, as they

had the toolkit out, took a look at the kitchen cabinet doors and got them hanging exactly right and shutting effortlessly.

"Anything else need doing?" Bill asked.

"No. I attend to DIY stuff on Wednesday mornings when Jenny's out having her hair done."

"So we can watch the football?"

"If you like, or go for a drive."

"I'd like to do that. Can't remember the last time I just went off somewhere without having it all planned out and having to be at a certain place on time."

Did Laura never stop talking? Jenny hadn't been able to concentrate on any of her programmes because of her chatter. She really wished Bill had a shed she could banish his wife too. If they could just get involved with the drama on the TV she could forget her disaster in Laura's kitchen. Of course that was her own fault. After Laura's paella she'd felt compelled to try something adventurous herself and attempted a soufflé. Too late she remembered Laura hated cheese and had substituted sautéed vegetables. The result was decidedly bland and incredibly difficult to wash out of the dish once they'd finished eating. It was a lot less stressful cooking for George who ate anything and would never make her feel her favourite recipes were too ordinary.

And where was George? He'd phoned in the morning to say he and Bill were going out for a drive and didn't know when they'd be back so not to worry if they didn't answer the phone. She'd rung every hour from lunchtime onwards without reply.

George and Bill decided they shouldn't really have fish and chips every night.

"The girls wanted us to realise how much they do for us, so maybe we should try making our own dinners?"

"I'm game if you are."

George did have to ring his daughter a couple of times, but they managed to make themselves sausage and mash one night and a cottage pie the next. They bought a cherry pie but made the custard they smothered it with.

"Reckon we're doing all right, George."

"Reckon so, Bill. How about we tackle the washing machine next? Don't want them to have a week's worth of laundry on top of getting us back."

Jenny hadn't thought she'd ever get bored of shopping, but the unthinkable had happened. As they'd already spent a day looking at every women's shoe and item of ladies attire they visited all the other shops on their second day. On the third they tried another mall further away, but it had the same shops as the local one.

"Shopping is better when you've got something special to shop for," Laura said. "If we were going to a wedding or something..."

"I suppose we could make a start on our Christmas shopping?"

Five days into their holiday the girls agreed they'd left the poor boys on their own long enough.

"They must be desperate for something decent to eat," Laura said.

"And bored without us there to organise them."

"And missing us of course."

"Of course."

They rang to give the good news. They had to leave a

message.

George and Bill had spent so long in the WW2 museum they'd had to be told it was about to close. On the way home they stopped for a pub meal, so didn't see the light on the answerphone flashing until quite late.

"I expect it's the girls worrying about us," Bill said.

"Won't they be relieved to know how well we're coping?"

"Sure will."

They listened to the message in silence. After a brief discussion about how they should proceed they decided it wasn't too late to call back.

When Jenny returned home she was surprised to see George had put the wrong bin out. That wasn't like him at all. As he carried in her bags she took a look inside. The bin was full of nothing but chip wrappers. She'd better make him one of his favourite meals tonight to make up for not having had a proper meal for days. She was surprised too that George and Bill were so keen to repeat the experiment.

"Now we see how much you do for us and how poorly we cope on our own, we think you deserve regular breaks from us. Maybe you and Laura can stay here and I'll go over to Bill's?"

She wasn't surprised to discover a big pile of dirty laundry waiting for her. She was puzzled though that it all seemed clean except for exactly the same greasy mark on each item. Almost as though chip papers had been rubbed on clean clothes. Still it was comforting to realise he needed her just as much as she needed him. She'd make him feel useful and ask him to take a look at the kitchen cupboards. She'd wait until he was going out to the shed so it would be easy for him to remember to bring his toolbox in.

George and Jenny waved goodbye to Bill and Laura. "Drive carefully," Jenny called, although Bill and Laura had already shut their doors and the engine was running.

"See you soon," called George although the other couple were too far away to hear.

"Not too soon though?" Jenny suggested. "I like being here looking after you."

"And I like you being here, my love. We'll leave it for a couple of months, shall we?"

Bill and Laura had a similar conversation as they drove away. Bill too agreed with his wife that she shouldn't go on another little holiday for about two months. Neither women realised that was just when the new Grand Prix season started.

13 Hallowe'en Candy

It was a cold, bright moonlit night. The children pulled on woolly hats, bright scarves and cosy mittens to go trick or treating. Their breath condensed into fog and their eyes sparkled with anticipation.

The kids all knew they were never to visit old Myrtle's cottage. Not at any time but especially not on Hallowe'en. Nobody told them why. The parents and grandparents should have done, then the kids wouldn't even have considered creeping down that dark, damp lane to see the lanterns glowing in her porch. Maybe people thought the collective guilty memories of stealing young Myrtle's candy would have seeped down through the generations. Maybe they thought the terror at their realisation of how huge a mistake that was, could be passed on through their genes.

So the kids only knew they weren't to go. They'd half overheard whispers of legends. Stories of the terror that awaited any child from the village who took candy from Myrtle on all hallows' eve. So they laughed, nervously it's true, but they laughed and crept, inch by inch, down the lane to take a look.

They saw the pumpkin lanterns, glowing warmly orange on her porch. They'd have looked welcoming if it hadn't been for the eerie shadows flitting around the garden. The kids stood still. A tall fair-haired boy kicked out, apparently by accident, at the ankle of his younger brother, sending him reluctantly forward. He stumbled, then laughed and pointed up into the leafless trees. Huge furry toy bats dangled on wires from the branches. Both the lanterns and carefully placed coloured lights illuminated the beasts. A gentle breeze sent silent shadows racing through the gloom. The children sniggered, embarrassed at their own fear. They crept closer to Myrtle's cottage.

Ghostlike shapes hovered, faintly glowing along the pathway. There was some shoving and shuffling until a plump girl stretched out a stripy mitten and slapped at the nearest ghoul. The sheet billowed, revealing the untidy bush beneath. She jabbed her woolly fingers at the crudely painted vacant face. No sniggers now, but real laughter.

As they stepped nearer, scents wafted out from Myrtle's open window; hot sugar, warm chocolate and rich caramel toffee.

One girl, tall with pigtails swinging, bounded up the steps to tap on the door. The other kids were close behind.

A metallic rattling was heard and then a creak as the door was unbolted and opened just a sliver. A delightfully horrible groan croaked out as the door swung open enough for Myrtle to peer around it. First they saw her hooked nose, then the white streaked quiff of her night-black hair. A beady eye was soon in view, followed by hairy warts and evil smile. Myrtle moved soundlessly into view. She'd taken as much trouble over her pentangle spangled dress, cobwebby cloak and pointed hat as she had with the make-up.

"Trick or treat, trick or treat," the children chorused innocently, gleefully.

"A bit of both my dears, a bit of both," Myrtle responded. Her voice too was gleeful. "Wait just a moment."

These children, unlike their forbears, waited to be offered the candy. They didn't know the truth, but they knew their manners.

Myrtle swiftly returned with a tray of handmade confections, crafted to her own very special recipe. As the children reached for sweet treats, Myrtle told them a story. The story they should have known. It was wonderfully gruesome and told with great conviction. They gasped, exclaimed and helped themselves to chocolate eyeballs and caramelised sugar fingers. In the centre of the platter was a gingerbread figure. A small thin arm reached towards it. A bigger boy's hand slapped it away and he took the biscuit from his little brother.

The children ate and urged Myrtle to tell them more. Only for a moment did they pause to notice each eyeball they picked up had been carefully iced in a shade exactly matching their own irises; blue or grey, hazel or brown. The caramel of each finger had been heated just enough for the resulting treat to take on a colour identical to their own skin tone. Even the nails, bitten, ragged or neatly trimmed were accurate.

Once the children closed their mouths around the confectionary, the sweetness faded and the treats dissolved far too quickly. Greedy for another taste, they forget their manners and snatched at more.

At first they hardly noticed the colours of the lights and warm glow begin to dim and recede as their world gradually darkened. They understood the stickiness though, as their mittens filled with blood. They screamed, of course, and ran off across Myrtle's spooky garden and down the lane. Straight home each child went, up into their beds and under blankets where it was supposed to be dark, where not seeing was all right.

They stayed there, quiet but not sleeping, until dawn broke. They saw the light coming through their windows. They saw their fingers clutching the blankets around their little bodies and counted. All were there, right where they were supposed to be. When they reached out they could feel the smooth cotton of their pillows, the soft fluff of their teddy bears.

Once out of bed they were able to see their parents, though not to say what had happened, or perhaps just seemed to happen. Maybe they had slept and it was just a dream.

Every child saw their parents' smiles and felt breakfast spoons tightly grasped in their hands. They saw and felt everything they were supposed to. All except for one small boy who felt the emptiness in the chair next to his where his older brother had always sat. He looked for the bigger boy. Everyone did, but not a single person had seen him since he ate gingerbread in the garden outside Myrtle's cottage.

14 A Girlie Girl

Emily gripped the paddle, her knuckles as white as the foam on the water. Her canoe crashed through the torrent while adrenaline pumped through her veins. The smile on her face was as bright as the sun sparkling off the icy river. It wasn't really happening though. She'd been staring at the computer for so long, trying to delay the coming ordeal, that her screen-saver had come up. There was no getting out of it, adventures like her latest white-water rafting trip were firmly behind her. Instead, Emily had to make do with tedious, girlie stuff like shopping.

"I'm going up town," she announced. "Can I get anyone anything?"

"No thanks, Em," Lucy said.

Charles, the deputy manager, offered to come with her. "I know you're getting Bill's present and thought you might like a hand carrying it."

"Kind of you. I'll be fine. Thanks." She grabbed her purse and rushed out.

Talking to Charles made her feel hot. Silly really, he was always pleasant and 'Expedition Em' as she was known at work wasn't the sort to get in a state over a man. Men didn't get in a state over her either. That kind of attention was reserved for the likes of her friend 'Luscious Lucy'. Emily had to change or no man would find her attractive; especially not the one she wanted.

Boyfriends lost interest when they learned her idea of fun

80

was scaling a cliff face or pot holing. Emily must get used to watching romantic comedies and putting on a skirt for dancing. That horrified her only slightly less than the idea of being permanently alone. At least she didn't have to change her job or her friendship with ultra-feminine Lucy.

Because Emily passed round the collection envelope she did nearly as much shopping as other women. She was good at persuading people to part with money, especially Charles. He was generous and thoughtful. He often offered her a lift to social events arranged by her colleagues even though her home was nowhere near his. She didn't like to inconvenience him so always refused.

Emily's pace slowed as she passed a cafe. Occasionally she'd bump into Charles outside. He'd stop and chat. Her part of the conversation consisted of nodding like an idiot and showing him what she'd bought.

"You must be hungry after all that shopping. Will you join me for lunch?" he might say.

"No. Sandwiches, I brought sandwiches," would go her reply.

The exchanges always left her confused. She didn't know why they happened, or how to react.

Usually Charles brought sandwiches to work and ate at his desk. He did a crossword and asked her to help. She liked that. She only had to say one word when she'd worked out an answer.

Emily needed to concentrate on gifts, not Charles. It would be her thirtieth birthday soon. Her gift would probably be awful. An envelope was circulating. She knew the signs. Charles had tactfully asked questions about things she might like. Her difficulty in talking to him meant she'd blurted out rubbish.

Bill's leaving present would be appropriate. He'd made no secret of his love for writing, so Emily bought a classy pen. There was money left. Usually she'd force herself to buy silly 'fun' items, but Bill didn't do silly. She grinned. Shopping for Bill wasn't really shopping at all; it was just buying stuff. Emily could do that. She set off to choose wrapping paper.

Paper! Writers need paper. Emily negotiated a great deal on boxes of plain paper. Too good; she couldn't carry it all.

"Get everything you wanted?" Charles asked.

"Yes, no. You were right," she mumbled.

"What was I right about, Emily?"

"The carrying. I couldn't... Would you...?"

"Of course. What is it you'd like me to collect from where?"

Luckily Charles generally seemed to understand what she was trying to say and soon extracted the details from her.

"Come on then, we'll take my car," he said.

Emily didn't know why he still needed her if he was driving but was too tongue-tied to ask.

She approved of his car. Although there was enough space in the back for the kind of bulky gear Emily needed on days out, it was compact enough to easily drive down country lanes. The bright blue was nice too.

"You like my car?" Charles asked as he unlocked it.

"Yes, nice colour." See, she could do girlie thoughts if she tried.

When Charles slid in next to her she realised the car was smaller than she'd first thought. His strong thigh was close to her own leg and his hand brushed against hers as they fastened their seat belts. Emily felt hot again and busied herself looking for the switch to open the window.

Bill was delighted with his gifts. "I'll dedicate my first book to all of you," he promised.

He returned to work on Friday. At first Emily wondered if he'd somehow forgotten he'd retired, but when everyone gathered around her desk, she realised he'd come in just to wish her a happy birthday. She had such a lump in her throat she couldn't speak. That didn't improve when Charles presented her with a bunch of flowers and kissed her cheek.

"Happy birthday, Emily."

"Lovely," she murmured. "I mean the flowers, they're lovely." They actually were. Instead of soppy pink roses, she'd been given metallic blue, spiky Eryngiums surrounded by bold foliage. They'd look good in her flat. Really brighten the place up. "Thank you, everyone."

Her legs seemed to have forgotten how to hold her up. She sat on her desk before she pitched forward into Charles's arms.

"Actually, this is your present from us," Lucy said, holding out a beautifully wrapped box. "I hope I got it right."

What did she mean? If the flowers weren't from all her colleagues then who...? She looked up to see Charles was the same red shade as her face must be.

Lucy tactfully gave her a nudge.

"Oh, yes. Thanks."

Emily knew what was in the box. It was the same size and shape as one she'd bought a few months earlier. That contained Lucy's favourite, ridiculously expensive, truffles. Flowers and chocolates wouldn't have been her first choice, but it was her own fault for not letting anyone know what she really wanted. The bouquet was gorgeous though and she liked chocolates.

"Thank you very much," she said again as she accepted the gift.

It couldn't be chocolates; it was far too light. Emily unwrapped it slowly. She wanted to be ready with a convincing smile when she opened the box. Her colleagues had joined together to give her something, that's what mattered, not what the gift actually was.

When the wrapper was removed it revealed a chocolate box. An empty one. Was it some kind of joke?

"Go on then, open it," Lucy urged.

Emily did and found a tiny red envelope inside.

"I've kept the receipt in case it's not what you wanted, but I've been reliably informed... Open it will you and put me out my misery?"

Emily couldn't help feeling sympathy for Lucy. She always had a moment of panic before people opened their gifts in case it wasn't what they wanted. Maybe the two of them were more alike than she'd realised?

She ripped open the envelope. "How did you know?"

Lucy nodded toward Charles. Emily couldn't remember telling him about her wish to go hot air ballooning, but she must have.

"Thank you, everyone. This really is exactly what I wanted."

"You're sure, Em? You can swap it for a spa day if you like."

Everyone laughed, Emily included.

"No thanks, Lucy, but if it makes you feel any better I'll put on some lipstick before I get into the balloon."

"Excellent idea. I'll come with you at lunchtime to help you chose it."

"There's no rush."

"I think there is," Lucy said. She walked away.

Nearly everyone had disappeared. Usually a couple of people sloped off to the kitchen at this point to bring out cakes. It didn't need all of them though. There had to be another reason she and Charles were alone in the office.

"There's sort of a rush, Emily. As it's your birthday tomorrow I've provisionally booked a flight for you. It can be changed if it's not convenient, but the man I spoke to said now was the perfect time to visit the forest."

"Forest. I, um..."

"Yes, it's quite a long way and you'll probably not want to drive after the excitement of your ride. I'd be very happy to drive you."

"Oh."

"If it's OK with you, I thought I'd follow and maybe take some pictures?"

"Oh, right. I expect everyone would like proof I really did it."

"And I'd like to take you to dinner afterwards. That's if you're free and would like to come?"

Oh help, what was she supposed to do now? She was used to him being kind, but this was more than that. Being asked out to dinner was something that happened to women like Lucy. Emily could see Lucy now, through the glass partition separating the office from the kitchen. Lucy was nodding her head. Emily found herself doing the same.

"Excellent, then it's a date," Charles said. He gestured for everyone to come back in with the cakes, saving her the embarrassment of further conversation.

Emily knew she was different from other women; surely not even the girliest of girls had ever felt as happy as this.

15 Everything Is Fine

What I did in the holidays.

One day we went to a big house called Grey Court or something like that. The house wasn't grey and I didn't see a tennis court even though there was a sign for one. The day out wasn't for me it was for Mummy. It was her birthday. That's why we just looked at a house and greenhouses and went for a walk instead of doing something proper like I would have chosen. I would have liked to play tennis because I want to learn to do that and be at Wimbledon and get strawberries and cream every day for tea and not have to eat eggs.

Before Mummy's birthday, Mummy and Daddy were talking. They weren't talking afterwards. Before Mummy's birthday other people talked to her and said it was nearly her big four roe. I asked Granny what that was and she said it meant she was going to be forty and Mummy's life would start then. Mummy is already alive but grown-ups are silly and say silly things. It was silly of people to tell Mummy about the big four roe. She smiled at them but I could tell she didn't like them saying it. You're supposed to say nice things to people when it's nearly their birthday, like they will get presents and have a party. Everybody knows that.

Mummy and Daddy didn't like how they talked to each other. Neither did Granny and me. I don't know why they stopped talking like normal people or did not-nice talking if they didn't like doing it. They used to do proper talking all the time and they were all smiley. I was going to have a baby brother or sister but then Mummy was ill. She went to hospital and I stayed with Granny. When I came home they had changed their mind about getting a baby and they started doing the funny talking. Strange funny, not good funny like the joke about zebras I told you, Miss.

They talked like they were reading stuff out.

Daddy would say, "Are you all right?" but I don't think he wanted to know.

Mummy said, "I'm fine." She wasn't.

They didn't just ask whose turn it was to take me to school or get the shopping for tea. Daddy said things like, "Would you mind?" before everything or, "If that's all right with you?" afterwards.

Mummy said, "That's fine."

Then it was Mummy's birthday. A big four roe birthday isn't like a normal grown up's birthday when you just get cards and a present at breakfast time and then it's all over. It's a proper birthday that lasts all day just like mine do. Mummy got lots of cards and presents and she tried to do smiling. There was a big cake but no party. I think that's because Mummy doesn't go to school so she wouldn't know anyone to invite to a party. Daddy said he was taking us out for the day and that he was sure it would do her good.

"Please come, my love," he said.

Mummy nodded her head. She didn't say fine, but I think she wanted to.

Mummy liked the present I made her. It was a purple terrordacktoll dinosaur to go in her bath. I explained how Daddy had helped me with the special glue so it wouldn't fall apart when it got wet. Mummy was very pleased about that and did real smiling and hugged me.

Daddy gave her a necklace. It was just a normal one and didn't have anything good like a plastic flower for squirting people but it was very shiny and she let Daddy do it up for her. Daddy's cold hands must have got a bit better because Mummy didn't jump so much when he touched her.

"Thank you, it's lovely," Mummy said. Lovely is better than fine.

We got in the car and Daddy drove us to the big house. It was a long way so Daddy played a CD. Daddy and I sang. Mummy didn't, but she didn't ask us to turn it off after five minutes and sometimes she turned round to smile at me. When we got there, Daddy parked the car in a field.

A man dressed like an orange gave us little tickets to get into the house. We couldn't go in straight away so we looked at the garden a bit. It was really boring. There were flowers but I wasn't allowed to pick them for Mummy like I do at Granny's house. There were apples and plums on the trees but I wasn't allowed to eat them. I wasn't even allowed to pick up the ones that had fallen off.

Daddy said there was a maze but when I asked if we could go to it he said, "I can't find the way."

He thought that was very funny. I didn't. Nor did Mummy.

"Aren't you enjoying yourself, Toby?" Daddy asked.

"It's fine," I said, just like Mummy did.

Daddy looked like something really scary had happened. Mummy looked like she might cry. I knew I'd done something wrong and I ran away. That's being like a little kid but I couldn't help it. There were lots of hedges and gates in the garden and I got lost. I thought it might be best to go back to the car. Even if Mummy and Daddy were cross with me I didn't think they would want to leave me behind so they might be happy to see me waiting when they wanted to go home and not be cross anymore.

The man who was dressed like an orange saw me and asked if I was all right. I didn't say fine. I cried and said I'd lost Mummy and Daddy. The man had a walkie-talkie and he talked on it about me. Another man came to give out the little tickets. His coat was the orange colour as well but he wasn't a very good orange because his tummy wasn't round. I didn't tell him.

The first man said he would help me look for Mummy and Daddy. He asked what they looked like but all I could remember was Mummy's necklace. If she had brought her dinosaur that would have helped people look for her because it was the only one like it. We walked along this big path and through a gate. Then I heard shouting.

Sorry, Miss, but my hand is tired and Mummy says it's bedtime now. I will right the rest tomorrow.

Part 2

So anyway, I had got lost at the grey court which wasn't a grey place and the man who looked like an orange was helping me look for Mummy and Daddy. We did some looking, then heard shouting is where I had got to.

"Toby! Toby!"

It was Mummy and Daddy. They weren't cross I had run away. I was right, they didn't want to go home without me. They liked the man dressed like an orange a lot. He went nearly the same colour as his coat when Mummy kissed him. Daddy wanted to give him a drink but the man said he was just glad they had found me and couldn't take it. I think he had to say that because he could see Daddy didn't have any cans of drink with him.

Then we all just stood there and Mummy said she thought we should go home. It wasn't the end of Mummy's birthday and I thought she wanted to see inside the big house so I tried to think of the right thing to say so they wouldn't go home yet. Daddy had thought not finding the maze was funny so I told the orange man about that.

The man smiled when I told him. "It's the other side of the big wall near the tower," he said. Then he had to go back to giving out the little tickets so other people could look at the house. He shook hands with Mummy and Daddy and me and said he hoped we would enjoy the rest of our day.

"Shall we look for it then, Toby?" Mummy asked me.

The maze was flat on the ground. At first I thought it was silly because you could see straight to the roundy thing in the middle which is what you're supposed to find. Daddy explained it wasn't as simple as it looked because I had to stay on the path and not jump over the bits of grass. He was right. I ran really fast but I couldn't get to the middle. Mummy and Daddy stood on the edge and tried to tell me which way to go. They weren't very good at it and kept telling me the wrong way and then they laughed when I ended up on the outside again and not in the middle. When I did get to the roundy thing they didn't even notice until I shouted because they were doing kissing. It was gross. I jumped over the bits of grass on the way back out because you're allowed to do that.

I was really hungry then and asked if it was lunchtime. It wasn't, it was the time we were supposed to go and look at the house. The house was OK, but not grey. It is made of bricks and is brick coloured. It was very old and we saw where servants would cook lots of dinners which made me even more very hungry. There was a place where children pretended they were at school but it didn't look like a school. Mummy and Daddy looked at absolutely everything until I was too hungry to look at a single other thing.

Lunch was a pie in a box. There were leaves and flowers in the box with it. Mummy ate all her leaves and flowers. Daddy didn't until she said it was good for us. Then we both had to eat them. The leaves tasted leafy and so did the flowers. We had ice cream for pudding. I had strawberry and cream flavour because Granny told me that if I want to play tennis at Wimbledon I will have to practise and they do eating strawberries and cream at Wimbledon. Mummy had a cup of tea. Daddy had coffee and he put in three sugars. I had apple juice and a red straw.

After lunch we looked round the garden a bit more. It was still boring but Mummy was smiling now and she was doing proper talking with Daddy so I pretended I liked it. Then we climbed up the tower. It was really high and cool like a castle. We could see everything from up there. I told them I was enjoying myself which was true up the tower. Mummy said she was too. We had a group hug then I thought they were going to do more kissing so I said I needed to go to the toilet.

There was lots more things to see but my hand is getting tired again with all the writing so I will just make a list. You can look them up on Google if you like, Miss.

1 Donkey wheel

2 Horse wheel

3 Ice house (don't look that one up because it's just a shed thing and not very good)

4 Moon gate

5 Evil ruins

6 Red Kites (if you guess what they are you will get it

wrong)

7 White garden

8 Pond

9 Tennis court (but we didn't find it)

That's all I can remember.

We said goodbye to the man dressed as an orange and I told him I didn't get lost again except a bit in the maze, but Mummy and Daddy could still see me so it was OK. He said that was good. Then we got in the car and Daddy drove it out the field and nearly all the way home. He played a CD again and we all did singing.

Mummy said Daddy should do silent singing because he was dreadful. That was a silly thing to say because you can't do silent singing because that's just being quiet and anyway Daddy is good because he knows all the words and sometimes some extra ones as well.

Daddy said, "My singing is better than Toby's."

Mummy said, "That's not difficult," but I think she was joking because she laughed.

When we were nearly home Daddy said, "Perhaps Toby might like to go and see Granny for a while this evening?"

He wasn't asking me, he asked Mummy.

Mummy said, "That's a good idea, how about it, Toby?"

I wasn't sure. It's nice at Granny's but Mummy had a great big chocolate birthday cake and I thought we might be having that for tea. Mummy promised she would save the cake until I came home so I said I would like to go to Granny's.

Poor Granny! I fell asleep nearly as soon as I got there so she couldn't play any games with me or read me stories which is what she likes doing. When I woke up again she drove me home. I told her I would come again another day in the school holidays and we could play games then so she wasn't too sad. (I really did do that and Granny liked it.)

Granny didn't stay very long because I think it was after her bed time. I don't really know what Granny does when I'm not there but I don't think it's much except when she goes pot holing.

Mummy had saved the cake and she let me have some before I went to bed. Mummy and Daddy weren't talking. They just sat on the sofa with me and kept doing smiling at each other. Grown-ups are very weird.

Granny isn't weird but that's because she's not a proper grown-up. I told Daddy that once.

Daddy said, "What do you mean, Toby?"

I said, "Granny is just like a little boy who has lived quite a long time."

Daddy laughed a lot but he said I was right and that I should tell Granny. I didn't because I think she already knows. Granny knows a lot of things. I asked her about Mummy and Daddy doing the funny talking and about changing their minds about my baby brother or sister. Granny explained it all to me but I won't put it in this story because it is very sad. This is a happy story because even though I got lost and that was a bit scary I mostly did have a good time.

Mummy had a good birthday and maybe Granny was sort of right about her life starting now because she is happy now. Daddy is happy too. Granny has gone pot holing again. I am happy even though I still don't know how to play tennis and all Mummy's chocolate birthday cake has gone. We will all live happily ever after. The very end.

Patsy Collins

16 Forget Me Not

Every time I see the picture of Gran, I wonder about the brooch. It's a pretty little silver thing, shaped like a forget-me-not and decorated with tiny blue glass beads. Despite what's happened, I don't see how it can influence anything.

Gran gave it to me after a boyfriend dumped me. Only Gran and my friend Chris seemed to care. It's a shame they never met, they'd have got on so well.

"Real love is worth waiting for," Gran reminded me.

Chris hugged me.

"You'll always have me," he said.

Gran claimed the brooch would help me find the right man.

"It did for me, Mazie love."

Granddad made it for her. His metalwork skills were needed during the war and he'd been called up before he found the nerve to propose. He'd worked long hours on the war effort, yet still spent his free time searching for materials and constructing the brooch.

Gran had missed him. As a way to show she was thinking of him, she'd hemmed a square of linen to make him a handkerchief. In one corner, she'd embroidered a tiny forget-me-knot. She received the brooch a few days after sending him his gift. She'd checked the leftover scraps of embroidery silk in her work basket against the beads; a perfect match, just as they were.

94

Whenever I'd been seeing a man for a while and began to wonder if things might get serious I'd wear the brooch. The first time I did, the man concerned asked me to remove it. He'd said it was cheap costume jewellery, a bit tacky and it might damage his designer suit. I didn't remove the brooch. I removed myself from him.

The next time I wore it, my latest love admired it. He said it brought out the blue of my eyes. When we kissed it brought a hanky out of his lapel pocket, along with his wedding ring.

When I tried again the man offered to buy it. I explained my attachment to it. He asked what was that compared to a good profit? I compared him to a few things, none of them pleasant.

I thought I'd never find the right man. I remembered how, when we were children, Chris told people we'd get married. He claimed we were meant to be together. He called me Maz, together we'd be ChrisMaz; for us it would be Christmas every day. Then I got old enough for boyfriends and he didn't say it anymore. I wondered if he still felt like that. When we next went for a drink, I wore the brooch. It seemed the thing was a jinx, destined to ruin every relationship I had. The man, who for years had been my reliable friend, spent an hour staring at my chest.

"I'd always thought better of you than that," I told him.

"Sorry it's that brooch, where did you get it?"

I explained it had been given to Gran and that she'd given it to me. I nearly said 'to bring me love', but changed my mind and said it was lucky.

"I met an old lady a while ago who'd dropped a brooch just like it. I found it for her. Then she said I should look out for it," Chris blushed, "because one day it would bring me love."

I thought it strange that a similar brooch would have the same kind of claim made about it. We discussed this and decided that perhaps there was some old wives' tale attached to forget-me-nots. We laughed and joked about our childhood 'romance'. Gradually we realised we both wanted to try it for real.

After a week or so, I introduced my 'new' boyfriend to Mum and Dad.

"Well thank goodness the pair of you have seen sense at last," Dad said.

Mum just smiled. If it was that obvious, why hadn't they bothered telling me?

Chris saw the picture of Gran. He picked it up.

"Do you know this woman?" he asked.

It was such a peculiar question and his expression was strange.

"Is something wrong?" I asked.

"She's the lady I told you about, with the brooch like yours."

"It can't be, that's my gran."

"When do I get to meet her? I want to thank her for what she said that day."

"I'm afraid you can't; she's dead," I said. "A stroke, I thought you knew?"

"I do remember your gran died whilst I was away at college, but surely that must have been your other grandmother."

"No, the gran who gave me the brooch died three years ago."

"But I saw her in April."

It doesn't seem possible that two women, who look alike, could have identical handmade brooches and believe, correctly, they'd lead to love. I might never understand, but it seems right to wear the brooch today. I pin it to my wedding dress and set off for the church, where Chris is waiting.

17 Picture Perfect

"Nan, I honestly don't think the two of us are going to be able to move the piano on our own." It had been a struggle for the three men from the second hand shop to get it into Nan's pick-up truck so Tess felt her concerns were justified.

Her grandmother just shrugged as she put the truck into gear. "Maybe we'll have help."

"Oh?"

"Next door's roses are looking particularly good. As good as a picture in fact and the weather is perfect, wouldn't you say?"

"Well yes, but I don't see how that'll help us shift a piano." The trouble was, Tess had a horrible idea that she did see. "No, not Matt? You can't still be taking advantage of him?"

"Would I do a thing like that?"

Tess grinned. "Most definitely."

"If you ask me, you're the one mistreating him."

"Well, I didn't ask you." But Nan was right, wasn't she? Tess hadn't been fair with Matt when she'd challenged him to take a perfect shot of the beautifully quaint street where her grandmother lived. At the time though it had just seemed a sensible precaution.

Matt was a photographer whom Tess had met at college; a popular joker who'd wanted to date her. She'd really liked him but didn't want to be his latest conquest who'd just get her heart broken when he moved on to the next girl. She'd said she'd be happy to go out with him, but not until after he'd shown her his perfect photo. She'd thought if she held his interest all the time it would take him to achieve that then she could accept he was serious about wanting a relationship with her.

Nan's street was a fantasy English village in miniature. It was mainly composed of pretty flint cottages, some with thatched roofs, and all with colourful gardens. It widened in the centre where there was a small pond. That was plentifully supplied with ornamental ducks and gracefully overhung by a weeping willow. The street even boasted a traditional red telephone box. It was no longer used to make calls and now maintained by local residents who used it to store the newspapers so the Scouts could collect them for recycling, but it still looked the part. Naturally the street was often visited by tourists, artists and photographers in search of the perfect shot Tess had challenged Matt to take.

It seemed an easy enough thing to do; with such a lovely subject how could anyone go wrong? Tess knew from experience something always occurred to make the task impossible. Hadn't she tried enough times herself? The minute she took the lens cap off something bizarre always happened. Rain would fall from a clear blue sky, a huge lorry would arrive with a delivery and block the prettiest part of the view or one of the residents would string up a washing line and hang out dozens of children's toys. She hadn't kept that information to herself either, but Matt had just laughed when she'd given him the warning.

"A good photographer works with things like that to capture a unique image, not uses it as an excuse for taking a poor one."

Tess hadn't been impressed with his smug assurance that he'd have no trouble doing what she'd failed to achieve and had enlisted Nan's help. She'd asked her grandmother to do all she could to sabotage Matt's pictures.

"How will I know it's him?"

"He's tall, got curly blond hair, bright blue eyes and lovely smile. He drives a cute little vintage car which is dark green with a cream canvas roof. He'll be completely charming to you and has the most amazing deep voice and..."

"Hmm, yes I quite see why you don't want to go out with him!"

"It's not that I don't want to, just that I don't want to get hurt again."

Nan squeezed Tess's hand. "I know, love. Don't worry, I'll do my best for you."

A few days later Nan had reported back. "Your young man came yesterday."

"He's not my young man."

"Whatever!" Nan had actually rolled her eyes and gestured with her hands like a fifteen-year-old. "I didn't have to do anything as it was bin day. There wasn't room for him to set up his tripod, let alone take a decent snap."

"Good. And you're sure it was him?"

"Oh yes, I went out and had a chat with him. You were so right about him. I tell you, if I was thirty years younger the poor chap wouldn't have had a chance."

"Oh, Nan!"

"OK, thirty-five."

"That's not what I meant and you know it. What did you say to him?"

"I was very discreet, don't worry. I like him though and think he'd be a good boyfriend for you. You're far too serious and he's fun."

Naturally the thought of Nan saying something she considered discreet did alarm Tess. "I hope you didn't say anything like that to him?"

"Now would I? Don't look at me like that, Tess dear. Maybe I might under certain circumstances, but I didn't, OK? I did encourage him to come back and try again though. That was OK wasn't it?"

"Yes. Thanks, Nan."

Matt had kept coming back and charmed all Nan's neighbours and Nan herself into agreeing he could photograph their homes and even themselves if he wished.

Nan reported she'd told him the street looked lovely all year. "Not that I needed to, he doesn't seem the sort to give up when he wants something."

That was good news for Tess, assuming he did still want her and hadn't just become interested in getting the photograph as a personal challenge.

Matt had helped prune roses and mend guttering as, by the time he'd set up his tripod, a ladder often appeared against the cottage he was hoping to photograph and helping was the quickest way to get it moved. The craftiest residents soon realised this and as a result Matt had put up decorations for a street party, mended cycle tyres and trimmed hedges.

After Matt told her about some of those incidents, Tess took pity on him and dropped hints that she might be willing to go out with him. They'd gone for a coffee a couple of times, but when her hinting switched to an outright acceptance of his previous invitation he'd turned her down.

"I haven't got that perfect shot yet, Tess. Once I have we'll go out together."

Tess had gone to visit her grandmother. "You can stop sabotaging his pictures now. I think he's proved that asking me out wasn't just a whim, so let him get the shot he wants and I'll agree to go out with him."

"Will you now? I'll have to see what I can do to help then, won't I?"

Unfortunately it had proved beyond Nan's powers to assist Matt in getting his one perfect shot.

The next time he visited Nan's street, a herd of escaped cows had invaded it. He'd helped get them out of gardens and later mend fences. Tess, alerted by a call from Nan, came to help and they'd all gone to the pub for a meal afterwards.

Since then Tess and Matt shared other meals but he always invited Nan too and he never gave her more than a peck on the cheek. It was very frustrating. Tess had long since decided his jokey manner was a good thing. He was always cheerful and pleasant, even when he was roped in to help clear the street for his shots. He must have known he was being conned, but seemed to enjoy the pranks that were played on him. Such a nice natured man wouldn't deliberately break her heart.

The worst of it was he wouldn't show her any pictures. She'd planned to say those shots depicting the bizarre things which happened in Nan's street did perfectly capture the place and he'd therefore completed his challenge. Her conscience would be clear as that would be absolutely correct, but how could she do it if he wouldn't show any of them to her?

Oh well, there was a more immediate problem to be solved. With hardly any crunching of gears Nan stopped her truck in the street. She leapt out and began untying the ropes which had held the piano safely in place. Tess got out too and looked around to see if Nan's guess was correct. It was; Matt was there looking eager to help. With the assistance of him and a couple of neighbours they got the piano into Nan's living room.

"Thanks for helping, Matt," Tess said.

"No problem. Come outside with me a minute will you? There's something I want you to see."

She followed him to his car, which was parked by the duck pond. It was then Tess noticed Matt didn't have his camera equipment with him. Surely he hadn't given up?

"It's a nice day for photography," she suggested. It really was and for once the street was peaceful, the oddest residents were out of sight, no lorries were attempting three-point turns, nobody was setting off for a fancy dress party and nothing was on fire.

"It is, but I don't think I'll be photographing this street again, not for a while at least."

"Oh." Tess made no attempt to hide her disappointment.

"You see, I've finished the project." Matt handed her a book. It was a huge hardback entitled 'The Perfect Shot' and it was a kind of photo documentary of the bizarre things that had happened in the street over the previous year.

Tess slowly leafed through it. It did perfectly capture the spirit of the place and people. Hallowe'en looked extra spooky in the fog, Christmas lights sparkled in the snow, the unfurling leaves of the willow and fluffy ducklings on the pond announced the arrival of spring and a curtain of roses decorated summer.

Matt had perfectly captured the crafty look of the one neighbour who always took advantage of Matt by fixing things in his front garden and also the grin on Nan's face as she brought Matt his tea and cake. Once, when up a ladder, he'd taken a shot of the neighbours all good naturedly laughing up at him. And there was one shot of her gazing at him from Nan's window; how she felt about him was shown perfectly. Her favourite image though was of a washing line full of teddy bears. Matt had caught them backlit with the sun so their fur was transformed into a magical glow.

"It's amazing, Matt. Perfect in fact."

"I'm glad you like it. I admit I started off wanting just the pretty picture and a date or two with a pretty girl, but gradually the charm of the place got to me and I wanted to photograph what was below the chocolate box lid."

"A right assortment!" one of Nan's neighbours said.

Tess looked round to see that all the neighbours had come out, led by Nan who told them all about Tess's challenge and the reason for it. Tess was fairly sure they'd heard the story before.

"So, Tess, what will it be?" Matt asked. "Dinner somewhere along the river so we can capture the sunset between courses, or a pub lunch followed by a long walk somewhere scenic, or perhaps you'd just like to come back to the studio for a drink and see what develops?"

"I, er..."

"Anywhere you like, just as long as you will come out with me?" Matt asked.

"Yes, yes I'd like that."

Matt kissed her as Nan and all her neighbours took photos on their phones and cameras.

18 Daffodil Days

As Dave raced down the road he half saw something. It niggled at him as he jumped onto the bus. As the vehicle transported him to work, he stared out of the window. He saw it again; a flash of yellow. Daffodils of course.

All the recent rain had made it grey and dark and he'd not seen them before. Once he realised what they were he saw them in almost every garden. They'd be in bloom everywhere, brightly trumpeting that spring was just around the corner, in all the gardens in the town. Even Julie's.

Once he got to work he saw more of them on a colleague's desk.

"Cheerful aren't they?" the woman said. "I always think there's something optimistic about daffodils."

That's what little Sienna had said. "Daffodils are cheerful flowers. Looking at them makes people smile."

He'd agreed back then. He was sure she'd get to see the daffodils flowering. Sure they'd all be smiling in the spring.

Sienna had cancer.

"She's in remission though," her mum Julie had told him not long after they'd started dating. She explained Sienna had needed chemo as a baby. The tumour had shrunk and stayed tiny and hopefully would go completely by the time she was a teenager.

Things hadn't worked out that way. It had grown again last autumn when Sienna was ten. She'd started on chemo and they'd been warned treatment would be a long and uncertain process.

Dave hadn't known what to do or say, but Sienna had a plan. "I want to plant daffodils for Mum. Whatever happens, she'll have something to smile about in the spring. Will you help me?"

He'd taken her, in secret, to buy plump bulbs.

"Can you get them to say 'I love you'? It'll be a message to Mum."

Sienna had been too weak to dig the holes, so he'd done that. He'd taken great care with the location of each and moved round the sack of bulbs so Sienna could place them carefully in. She was tired afterwards, but the smile on her face told him he'd been right to let her do it.

Dave wished there was more he could do to help. He wanted to hug them and promise it would be OK, but how could he when the doctors had given no such assurance? He couldn't pay for better treatment as he was barely keeping a roof over his own head. Couldn't say how he felt as this wasn't about him.

"I'm going to be with her," Julie said.

"I'll drive you to the hospital."

He took a day off work to do it and repeated the hundred and fifty mile journey at the weekend. They wouldn't let him in to see Sienna. "Immediate family only."

Julie came out to see him. "I'll be at the hospital all the time, Dave. I won't have time or energy for anything else. For anyone else."

"Of course." What right did he have to pull her away from her daughter, even for a few moments? He'd wanted to earn that right, to show he cared, but he'd left it too late. A hurried declaration of love in a hospital corridor would have sounded like empty words.

He went to her home several times while she was away. Keeping the garden tidy and checking the house was secure wasn't much, but it was all he could think of until he found the sketch Sienna had made for the placing of the bulbs. He bought another big bagful and planted those too.

The days got shorter and darker. Julie never mentioned his visits, perhaps she didn't spend enough time at home to notice. Dave received a Christmas card and thanks for the gifts he left. They exchanged a few texts which didn't say much. He worked every hour he could. If money could help Julie, or Sienna, then at least he'd have some to give. It didn't buy happiness, he knew.

Eventually Dave began to understand. Julie had been hurt before, just like he had. No, much worse. Sienna's father, the man they should have been able to rely on, had taken fright at Sienna's illness and left them. Why would she expect better of a man who'd not even found the courage to admit he loved her? Loved them? Julie hadn't been trying to push Dave away, she'd just been giving him an easy way out. Idiot that he was, he'd taken it.

Then he'd seen daffodils everywhere. An optimistic flower. One that made people smile. Had Julie seen the ones he'd planted with Sienna, the ones he'd added on his own. Had they made her smile? He hoped so.

He went to see. He hesitated on the pavement. He could see cards on the windowsill. It wasn't either of their birthdays. Get well cards? Sympathy ones? For a moment that easy way out looked tempting, but he walked up the path and knocked.

As soon as Julie opened the door he said, "I'm so sorry. I should have stuck by you. I love you, Julie."

"Still?"

"Yes. I should have told you."

"You did." She showed him the daffodils in bloom spelling out 'WE LOVE YOU'. The first word was a little squashed from where he'd added to the original 'I' but it didn't look too bad.

"Sienna?" he whispered.

"Upstairs. She's sleeping now, but she'll wake soon. You can see her then, if you like."

Dave felt relief flood through him.

"Julie, when I tried to visit her before they said immediate family only."

"That was only just after the first operation. She's almost well again, so it won't be a problem."

"Good, that's good, but it's not quite what I meant. I... I don't want that description to exclude me."

Instead of replying, Julie took his hand and led him into the garden. "Let's pick daffodils for Sienna's room."

She selected them carefully, handing each in turn to Dave. When she'd finished he saw she'd left, 'I LOVE YOU', in cheerful, optimistic blooms.

19 It Was Big And Green

Nine-year-old Adam was really enjoying his first day on the beat. He'd only spent fifteen minutes with his hero, PC Marks, but he'd already managed to assist three members of the public.

"You were quite right, Adam; you are useful to have around," the policeman said.

"Really and truly?"

"Oh yes, when your neighbour asked for the time, you'd given him the answer before I could even look at my watch."

"That's because I'd just checked mine to make sure I wasn't late. I wouldn't want to hold you up."

"Excellent. Punctuality is very important in police work."

"Could you spell that long word for me, please?" Adam asked as he took out his special note book.

PC Marks explained what the word meant and spelt it out for him. Adam wrote it down so that he'd remember it when he was old enough to be a real proper policeman himself.

"I was useful for carrying in Mrs Johnson's shopping as well, I think?" Adam asked.

"You were, and with giving directions to the library."

"That one was easy. I go there every week with my mum," Adam explained.

"To borrow books about the police force, I expect," PC Marks said.

"Yes, how did you know?" Adam was yet again impressed by how much the police officer knew about what went on in the village.

His hero made no comment but it looked as though the policeman smiled before he hastily turned away.

"Hello, what's all this then?" PC Marks said and pointed to an elderly man who was hurrying towards them and waving his arms.

"Officer, officer!" the man called out.

PC Marks and Adam, his trainee deputy, walked towards the man. Adam noticed it was a friend of his granddad's who everyone referred to as Old Bert, even though his name was Mr Grahame.

"I... I..." Mr Grahame tried to say.

"Take your time, sir," said PC Marks.

Mr Grahame took a few noisy breaths, pulled off his cap, wiped his head with a red and white spotted handkerchief, breathed some more and then stood up straight. "I wish to report a crime," he said.

"What kind of crime, sir?" PC Marks asked.

Adam hardly heard him; he was thinking that he might have to go home now. Mum and Dad and PC Marks had agreed that Adam could join the policeman when he walked the beat in Adam's village. There were conditions though. He could only do it at the weekends and only if he'd finished his homework. Also he'd had to promise that if there was a serious police matter, or anything dangerous happened, or if PC Marks said so for any reason, then Adam would go straight home.

"It was a theft!" Mr Grahame said.

Oh dear, Adam thought; theft is a serious police matter.

"Adam, I'm sorry, but perhaps you'd better go home

now..." PC Marks started to say.

"Let the boy stay," Mr Grahame interrupted. "His granddad told me all about how he helps the police. Maybe he can help me as well."

"I'll try, sir," Adam said.

"What is it that seems to be missing, sir?" asked PC Marks.

"My prize marrow and three old roller skates. I'm not worried about the skates, but the marrow is a different matter."

"A prize marrow, sir?"

"That's right. It won first prize in the biggest marrow competition at the local show. Adam here saw it, didn't you, boy?"

"Yes, I did," Adam agreed. "It was really, really huge; even bigger than my granddad's one and that was absolutely enormous."

"Right," PC Marks said. "Was the prize stolen too?"

"No, no. Just the marrow. My twenty-five pence prize and winner's certificate are quite safe."

"Twenty-five pence, sir? Was the marrow valuable?"

"To me it was. I had plans for that marrow."

"Can you describe it, sir?"

Mr Grahame blinked. "It was big and green and marrow shaped."

"Right. Did it have any distinguishing features?"

"Like I said, it's big. Very big. The biggest marrow anyone in the village has ever seen before."

PC Marks nodded.

"But I think it might be damaged now. There were a few pieces of what looked like marrow skin on the ground."

The policeman looked confused, as though the crime had baffled him. Adam wished he could help, but he couldn't think who might have stolen the marrow. Granddad had made a joke about pinching it before the show so that Granddad and not Mr Grahame would win the prize, but Adam knew that Granddad hadn't really meant it. Maybe someone not as nice as Granddad had the same idea? He shook his head, that wasn't right.

"It doesn't make sense," Adam said. "Why would anyone steal it after the show?"

"Good point, lad," Mr Grahame said. "I've got the prize now, but that still doesn't make it all right for someone to steal the thing."

"No, it doesn't," agreed PC Marks.

"It was wrong to take the skates without asking too, even if you didn't want them," Adam pointed out.

"Ah! Skates, hmm. Thanks for reminding me, deputy," PC Marks said.

Adam smiled. He loved it when his hero called him deputy; it made him feel important. He thought he might have said something important, although he didn't know what it was.

"I think I can sort this out," PC Marks said. "Let's start by visiting the scene of the crime and I'll take a few details from you on the way, sir."

"Fine," Mr Grahame said, "My name is..."

"Bert Grahame," PC Marks said before Mr Grahame had told him.

Adam gasped; the policeman was very clever. How did he know?

"That's right. How did you know?" Mr Grahame asked.

"I read about the village show in the newspaper. I

remember now, that when the vicar presented the prizes, he mentioned the marrow would be big enough to feed dozens of homeless people."

"That's right, officer," Mr Grahame said. "The reverend Grande did say that. But I..."

"And then one of the prize-winners offered to donate all of the vegetables on his allotment to the vicar's charity. That was you, I believe, sir?"

"Yes, but..."

"Very generous, sir."

"Well, not really. I'd already harvested quite a lot and my wife has made pickles and frozen as much as she can. I just thought it a shame to waste what was left. Surely you're not suggesting the vicar took my marrow?"

"Just considering the possibility, sir."

"Could he really have taken it?" Adam asked. It didn't seem right that Reverend Grande could be a thief.

"It'd be fine if he did," Mr Grahame said. "He did take quite a lot of the other vegetables. At least I assume it was him and not the marrow thief."

"It would seem reasonable that he'd take the marrow, then," PC Marks said. "As it was so large, it would have fed a lot of people."

"Perhaps I didn't properly explain how big the marrow was? The thing was huge. Reverend Grande would never have been able to lift it, never mind carry it back to the vicarage. He wouldn't have been able to get anyone to deliver it for him either, as he's given up using cars for a month to try and show people how to reduce pollution."

"Even so, I think perhaps we should speak to him, sir?"

Adam was amazed. He'd been so busy listening to what PC Marks was saying that he hadn't realised that instead of walking to the allotments, they'd gone to the vicarage. Mr Grahame looked quite surprised too.

PC Marks rang the doorbell. After only a short time, Reverend Grande opened the door and invited them all in.

"Do you have time for a cup of tea?" he asked.

"That's very kind of you, sir," said PC Marks.

"Yes, please," Adam said, politely.

"Very kind indeed," said Mr Grahame.

"Talking of kindness, Bert," Reverend Grande said. "Thank you so much for all the wonderful vegetables, especially that superb marrow. The ladies of the village are working hard to make them all into soup. I was going to call round later to return the skates, but as you're here now, perhaps you'd take them?"

PC Marks smiled, Adam gasped and Mr Grahame spluttered.

"I hope you didn't mind me borrowing them," the vicar continued. "You see that marrow was far too heavy for me to carry, so I hollowed it out, filled it with the other vegetables and tied on the roller skates so that I could use it as a wheelbarrow."

"I knew there was something odd about the skates going missing!" Adam said.

"Case closed, I think, deputy?" PC Marks asked.

Adam agreed it was and then everyone had tea and chocolate biscuits to celebrate.

20 Teacher's Pet

Rose had worried a little about taking her seat on the minibus. She hoped to sit where she could look at Mr Winters but didn't want to be too obvious about it. Then there was Liam. Should she make an attempt to sit with him or not? She decided not. She'd volunteered to help supervise the whole class, not just her son.

She needn't have worried. Matters were taken out of her hands. At the very last moment, one of the girls, Penny Carter, declared she needed the toilet. Rose had to run back into school with her. When they returned only two empty seats remained. Penny belted down the back of the bus to sit with her chum. Rose was left with the seat opposite the driver: Mr Winters.

During the journey he gave her titbits of information to pass on to the children.

"One of the things we'll see is an ice house. Can you guess what that is?" Rose asked.

After listening to their imaginative theories, she promised Mr Winters would explain the real answer later.

As he was driving, she could watch him without his being aware. Once she caught his gaze and blushed like a white rose touched by the sun. Fancying the teacher seemed almost akin to seducing one of the monks at the Abbey they were about to visit. Not that there were now any monks to seduce or that she had anything to be ashamed of. She was a member of the PTA not one of the kids. She was single and anyway didn't have much hope of seducing Mr Winters.

At one time she'd thought she did. She'd been flattered when he'd paid attention to her at a fund raising event, asking her to join him for a drink afterwards. He could have his pick of the yummy mummies, but it was always her he headed for whenever she went in to help with anything. Fortunately that was quite often. The small village school relied on volunteer help and Rose was one of the few whose job allowed her to provide it during the day.

As well as running a plant stall at the school fete, helping with the children's garden and going on trips, she'd been talked into taking the part of Cinderella in the school play. Traditionally that involved both staff and pupils writing the script, creating sets and costumes and acting the roles. The children had seen to it that the play included a lot of showering people in various items. First Rose was covered in fake soot and dust as she cleaned for the Ugly Sisters, then the whole cast were coated with fairy dust. Finally Rose, and Paul Winters as Prince Charming, had vast quantities of confetti thrown over them during the wedding scene.

Rose didn't mind and Paul seemed quite happy to rehearse all the scenes they shared. She'd waltzed in his arms at the ball, had him hold her foot to fit the shoe and been held tight during their fictitious wedding. She thought they'd given quite a good impression of a couple in love at the end.

"Please call me Paul," he'd urged.

"I'm not sure I should." She fancied him like mad but was determined not to behave inappropriately in front of the pupils, nor to make things difficult for Liam. Maybe she'd overdone it and hid her feelings from Mr Winters too? It had all gone wrong just at the moment she thought their relationship had been hotting up.

It looked like she'd have to settle for just friends. She was good at that as she'd learnt to do the same with Liam's dad Keith. He and Rose had both inherited shares in a garden centre and had worked together on the business. Rose had been young then, shy like a tightly furled bud. Things had got out of hand in the potting shed once, but the relationship cooled even before she'd realised she was pregnant. Keith did his best to be a good dad to Liam and a good friend to her. It could have been awkward, especially as they still owned the business together, but usually it was fine. With her son to love and her share in the business to develop, Rose had blossomed.

She'd explained a little of that to Paul Winters in the staff room one afternoon.

"It's good, for Liam that you and his father both get on so well and he spends time with both of you together."

"A lot of time. We're still partners."

She'd seen from his expression he thought she meant they were a couple, not business partners but before she could correct that idea the bell had rung for his next lesson. Ever since she'd been trying to drop into the conversation the fact she was single. She knew her attempts had been too subtle but didn't want to try a direct approach which would embarrass them both if he wasn't interested. She'd hate him to think of her as an overblown rose in need of deadheading.

The romantic gardens of Mottisfont Abbey seemed to be working their magic. Mr Winter relaxed as they allowed the children to run round in the grounds and let off steam. He told her more about the lives of those who'd lived in the house. Not in a lecturing about the Romans kind of way, but in a making her laugh till she had to hold onto him for support kind of way. He was so easy to talk to. A good person to have as a friend although she wanted a little more than that. A lot more, actually.

In turn she told him something of the history of medicinal plants and of the roses which were scenting the air.

"I guess with your name you'd either love roses, or never want to see one."

"I absolutely love them. I always did, but working on the nursery has made me much more knowledgeable. Liam's dad, my business partner, taught me a lot." She stressed the word business.

"Ah. I see... Do you sell a lot of rose plants?"

"Sadly not so many of the old fashioned sorts such as they have here. People don't often grow them now because the flowering period is much shorter than modern hybrids, but I think they have more charm despite that."

"Maybe because of it?"

"You could be right." Some things were better if they didn't go on for too long. Christmas and warm summer showers for instance. Not relationships though. She hoped that if she formed one with Paul she'd have more than a few heady weeks of pleasure before it was all over.

"Suppose we'd better get the kids back under control," he said.

They explored the house and learned about the priory from which it had been formed as well as the lives of more recent residents. After a picnic lunch under a shady tree the children grew restless again. Paul Winters had them seek out the well, then race to the ice house.

"These were used in the days before people had fridges or freezers to keep food cold. They put ice in here during the winter and stored it to use in the winter."

"Why didn't it melt, sir?"

"Go in and see if you can find out."

The boy did. "It's freezing in here!"

The rest of the class joined him to see if he was right. Afterwards, Paul Winter encouraged them to run alongside the river Test trying to keep exact pace with the fast flowing water. He and Rose watched them with their feet firmly planted on the rose covered bridge.

"I want to get a photo," Paul said. "Can you throw in a stick for them to chase?"

He left her side to take snaps of his class eagerly charging noisily along the river bank.

Once the children were calm enough to look without causing damage, Paul and Rose took them into the confines of the walled garden. They divided into groups so as not to block the narrow paths, but Rose could still hear Paul talking to his pupils.

"Do you have many roses like this at home, Liam?"

"Lots at Mum and Dad's work and some at Dad and Linda's house, but not where me and Mum live. Our garden hangs from the window."

"Excellent," Paul Winters replied. Rose doubted he was referring to her lack of growing space.

With an effort she pulled her attention back to her own group and encouraged the children to look for birds, butterflies and other wildlife among the plants.

"Look, look, Miss Rose," Penny Carter yelled.

Rose looked up to see a bridal party had come to have photos taken in the garden. She ushered the children out of shot as best she could, which meant her group rejoined the one Mr Winters was leading. The children watched fairly quietly until the guests showered the bride and groom with confetti.

"Oooh, sir it's just like you and Miss Rose in the school play," Penny Carter pointed out.

Paul Winters agreed it was.

"Do it now!" Penny's friend Freya urged.

Paul obliging stood close to Rose as the children threw a confetti of fallen petals over them.

"This does make a lovely setting for a wedding," she murmured.

He raised an eyebrow.

"Sorry, just thinking out loud. I didn't mean..."

"It's OK. You're right it's the perfect setting." He handed over his phone to show the pictures he'd taken when she was on the bridge. "Reckon you could pick a perfect bridesmaid too." Partly hidden behind the cloud of tiny white roses, Rose looked like a bride in a veil. Young Penny tugging at her skirt, illicitly picked flowers in hand, looked just like a bridesmaid holding her train.

"I couldn't choose just one," Rose said. "It would have to be nine bridesmaids and seven pageboys. Maybe it'd be better to elope?"

He grinned. "Hmm, I'll think about it but maybe we could start off with dinner?"

"Yes, good idea. I'm free on Saturday evening as Liam is going to the cinema with his dad," she said, eager to have something arranged before he was distracted.

"I'll pick you up around seven then. But before that I'd better stop acting like a newlywed and turn back into a teacher."

"I suppose," Rose said.

The children had other ideas though. Deciding they were all budding photographers, the class insisted on a dozen more pictures and a lot more confetti throwing.

21 What The Cat Brought In

The metal bird trailed from Fluff's mouth as he bounded through the cat flap. He presented me with a dangly silver earring. I wondered if he'd finally realised I wasn't the sort of chap who collected dead mice. That offering was certainly an improvement on them. There were numerous coloured droplets arranged to represent a peacock's tail. Held flat in my hand it didn't look much, but held by the hook and allowed to move and shimmer it was curiously lifelike.

Fluff sat on the cool tiles of the kitchen floor and awaited a fitting reward for his cleverness in hunting down such a cunning prey. He'd probably stalked around this trinket for long minutes before sensing the moment was right to pounce. I opened a tin of tuna and watched him eat. His dainty manners made him a very different cat to the one who first pushed his way through the cat flap, into my life.

That was the day I moved in. My possessions were still in packing boxes. I'd removed only the essentials, a toothbrush, razor, quilt and some beer. My pizza was delivered by the regulation spotty youth on a moped. When I carried it into the kitchen, Fluff was crawling through the cat flap. I called him Fluff because the only cat's name I could think of was Fluffy and he didn't have enough hair to qualify.

I didn't know what to do. He looked starved and it was raining, so I couldn't push him out into the night. It was late and I'd had a couple of beers so I couldn't drive him anywhere, even if I could have thought of anywhere suitable.

He was shivering. I opened a box hoping to find a tea towel to dry him with. The first thing I spotted was a tin of tuna; the kind with a ring pull. I tipped the contents onto the lid of the pizza box. Fluff ate it in three huge gulps.

In the morning, he was gone. I went shopping for milk, bread and fruit. I introduced myself to the neighbours and fell in love. I had met Mrs Davies before when I viewed the house. I knew she was a widow with a student daughter. I hadn't seen Lucy then. If I had, I wouldn't have haggled so much over the price.

It would be difficult to describe Lucy without making her sound ordinary. Long hair that's a sort of shiny brown colour, very large eyes that are almost blue, a large smiling mouth and a few freckles. The usual number of legs and arms all connected to a curvy, yet neat, body. See what I mean? That doesn't tell you what she's like. I'll just say that she looks joyful. Her whole body smiles. She's filled with laughter trying to escape.

I'm not good at judging girl's reactions to me but she didn't seem repulsed.

"I hope you like living here, Douglas, I do. There are lots of great places to go. You could do with someone local to show you around."

"I got a lot of information from the estate agents and a map."

"Oh, well, fine."

I was trying to decide between Indian and Chinese takeaways for supper when Fluff returned. There was plenty of tuna; I emptied a tin onto a plastic carrier bag and he ate greedily. I opened another can and he finished that too, but was eating slowly towards the end. I fished an empty yoghurt pot from the bin and gave him some milk.

Again, he was gone in the morning. Lucy was still next door, so I went calling.

"Do you have a contact number for the people who owned my house before?"

"Mum might have, she's certainly got the address if there's mail to send on."

"No, it's about their cat. It's found its way back home."

"You're being haunted? Cool."

"Haunted?"

"Yeah Sooty died last year."

"That's not right."

"No it's OK, he was really old. They were sad of course, but he'd had a good life, they said."

"Was he black?"

"Sooty? Are you having me on?" Her whole body shook with giggles, in a rather attractive manner.

"The cat that comes into my house late at night and scoffs my best tuna is nearly bald and scraggy looking, but he's not black and he's not dead."

"Can I see him?"

"He comes quite late."

"That's OK."

"Perhaps when his hair's grown a bit."

"Oh, well, fine."

She sounded put out, why would she would want to come to my house in the evening? Fluff isn't much to look at.

Fluff came for supper again that evening and was again gone by morning. I felt used. He turned up when he felt like it, got what he wanted and left. I thought of blocking up the cat flap. He wasn't my responsibility.

Saturday was the local fete day. That sort of thing doesn't usually interest me, but I thought I would see what the rest of the locals were like. There was also a chance Lucy might be there. I didn't expect her to be dressed as a serving wench and selling kisses.

She wasn't. She was dressed as a student and selling raffle tickets.

"First prize is a dinner for two at Luigi's."

"There's only one of me."

"I'm sure you could persuade someone to come with you. It's a lovely restaurant, I really like it there."

"I suppose I could take Dave from work."

"Oh, well, fine."

Again, Lucy seemed slightly annoyed. I didn't know why.

I didn't win the dinner or anything else in that raffle. I did win my choice of lipstick, a knitted doll or some cat food on the Girl Guides' tombola. It was not a brand I'd heard of. I was not then an authority on cat food, I am now and I've yet to see it for sale.

There was a fortune teller. She beckoned me in. I wasn't sure I wanted my fortune told, but she was sure she wanted to tell it.

"I see a pet, a nice soft-furred cat."

"That's not mine then."

"I see not what is, but what will be, young man."

Her attitude was perfect; haughty and superior. I had suffered hardships and triumphs, apparently. The mists cleared and she saw travel and great happiness. I would prosper and have many children. She put on quite a good performance, so when she suggested I cross her palm with silver to help the RSPCA I didn't mind feeding some coins into the collection box.

"Keep the cat. He'll find a way to bring love to whoever cares for him."

It was amazing how she knew about Fluff. She either had second sight or had spotted the hairs on my sweater and read the label on the tin I clutched.

As I came away from the fortune teller, I saw Lucy again. Now there, I thought, was a girl I'd like in my future.

"Shall I get some platform shoes, then?" she asked whilst standing on one leg with her thumbs in her ears. She's so lovely.

"Why would you want to do that?"

"Aren't you going to meet a tall dark stranger? I'm dark, the shoes would make me tall and I can be as strange as you like."

"Nah, it's OK thanks," I said, wondering why she would want to make herself taller. She seemed to already be the perfect height.

"Oh, well, fine."

Those words again, what had I done now?

Fluff came back that evening. He ate, slept and left. He was back again on Monday. I opened my hard won tin of cat food. He wouldn't eat it. I wasn't surprised as it looked like orange rice pudding and smelt of over-cooked sprouts. I decided to let him stay; I wasn't going to be bullied by him. He could eat the food or go hungry.

By morning, most of the cat food was still there. So was Fluff. He didn't look well. Worried I'd accidentally poisoned him, I asked Mrs Davies if she knew of any vets. She gave directions to McGregor's and Lucy offered to come with me to hold Fluff whilst I drove. I didn't want to put her to any trouble, but I did need help. I reluctantly agreed.

"Oh, Lucy, it seems silly to be so upset. He's not even really my cat and I've only been feeding him for a few days. I hope he doesn't have to stay in, I think I'd actually miss him."

"It just shows what a kind caring man you are, Douglas. You shouldn't stay at home and mope though. You should go out and have some fun, preferably with a companion who knows all about Fluff."

I was about to say I had a video I wanted to watch, when it occurred to me that Lucy was the only person who really knew about Fluff. Without realising it, she'd given me an opportunity to ask her out. Before I could, Fluff was called for.

There wasn't anything actually wrong with him, apart from his poor condition. The vet gave him a vitamin injection, some worm medication, checked that he wasn't microchipped and gave me advice on caring for him. I checked with the police and RSPCA that he hadn't been reported missing.

His hair grew back. Gradually he became a handsome animal. I fitted him with a collar and bell to stop him catching baby birds. The earring was the closest he came to that. It looked a bit art deco, could be valuable. I put it in the kitchen drawer, knowing it would be safe there and set off on my walk.

I'd taken to strolling round the village of an evening. The scenery was lovely, especially when Lucy was out sunbathing. She often chatted to me over the hedge. She told me of the pubs she went to with her friends. I wished she wouldn't, I'd have liked to ask her out myself, you see. She was always out with her friends. I guessed she wouldn't be interested in spending time with me. She told me about dances that were due to be held and that she was thinking of

126

going.

"Not the sort of place to go to on your own though."

"No I suppose not," I agreed.

"Great fun if you go with a friend."

"I'm sure you'll have fun, whoever you go with."

"Oh, well, fine."

I wished it was me she would be dancing with, but that was just a fantasy.

As I returned home, past the Davies's house naturally, I spotted Lucy crawling through her mother's shrub border.

"Are you OK?"

"Yeah, just looking for something."

"Want a hand?"

"Yes please. It's about so big and silver, blue and green." I tried to keep my attention on the ground and away from Lucy's T-shirt. Belatedly I realised that we should really be looking in my kitchen drawer. Well it was getting dark, I'd help her look for a bit longer then we'd have to give up. I'd come round the following day after work and 'find' it then. Perhaps she'd let me take her out for a drink as a reward.

The next morning, Mrs Davies spotted me.

"Have you come to help look for the earring?"

I nodded hoping she wouldn't help. I didn't want an audience when I 'found' it.

"I'm so glad, but could you wait for an hour?"

"I suppose so, but why?"

"Lucy will be back then. It would be better if you found it together don't you think?"

I wasn't entirely sure about that and began looking round for a suitable place to drop the thing. I wanted to be sure I was the one to discover it.

"The earring was given to Lucy by her grandmother as a lucky charm. It's supposed to find a way to bring love to whoever owns it."

I was reminded of the words of the fortune teller claiming that Fluff would find a way to bring me love.

"Don't worry, we'll find it together."

I meant the earring, but hoped love was part of the package.

All that was a year and sixteen days ago. We are back now, from our honeymoon. Mrs Davies, I can't get used to Mum, has been looking after Fluff. He now has a bald patch on his jaw.

"He was playing with Lucy's earring and somehow scratched himself. I was worried it might go septic, so I rushed him straight to the vet. David McGregor shaved off a bit of hair to clean the wound. I feel so bad; I should have looked after him better."

"He doesn't seem worried by it, he'll be fine. I don't blame you at all, he's fascinated by that earring," I assured her.

"That's one of the reasons I've given it to you, Mum," Lucy reminded her. "I don't want Fluff carting it off somewhere, but I'm also hoping it will bring you love, just like it did me."

"Mrs, er Mum, would you like to come out to dinner with us tonight, as a thank you for looking after Fluff and the house?"

"Sorry, Douglas, I can't. Fluff's vet, David McGregor, is taking me to Luigi's."

Fluff began to purr.

22 Stormy Weather

Mr Day, the producer of the local radio station, had been charming during Gail's interview for the position of weather presenter. He put her immediately at ease by saying, "Call me Ricky, please. We're pretty informal here." It wasn't long before he said, "Now, Gail, with a name like yours, I reckon it would be mad not to give you the job."

That lifted the dark cloud of nervous uncertainty and allowed Gail Rayner to shine.

"It is perfect for a meteorologist," she agreed.

"You realise you'll have to start early in the mornings?"

"I worked on a market stall twice a week to help support myself through uni, so I've had plenty of experience of early starts as well as different weather conditions."

"And the pay... you'd only be part-time so it's not a lot."

"True. It won't even qualify me to start paying back my student loan." She saw him wince at her tactlessness and added, "It's fair for the hours though."

It would feed her and pay something towards the rent on the house she shared with her sister. Plus she'd be doing the work she'd trained for and loved. The studio was warm and dry, she would have to get up before the morning dew formed, but would finish early and avoid the traffic jams.

"My only reservation about hiring you," the producer had said, "is that you're so attractive you'll be lured onto the television team and I'll have to replace you very soon."

"I want to get some experience and do a good job, that's more important to me that getting on television." She spoke more frostily than she'd intended. Several fellow students had seen TV weather presenting as a fast track to fame and fortune rather than providing a service.

He nodded as though convinced. "You did say you could start immediately? How about tomorrow? You could work with Jeff for his last few days to learn the ropes."

"That's wonderful. Thank you so much."

On her first day she was shown around the building, issued with her security pass and invited to sit in with Jeff as he read the weather report. Although she kept quiet she could see why Jeff was moving on; his heart clearly wasn't in the job.

On her second and third days Gail read out scripts Jeff had prepared. They were so vague she made sure to thank Jeff on air for producing them. Gail had no intention of being associated with such riveting stuff as 'it could be chilly in some places so wrap up warm' especially as the day turned out to be the warmest for several weeks.

Ricky appeared before or after several of her broadcasts to encourage or praise her as appropriate.

"Thankless task this," Jeff said on his last day. He showed her a sheaf of complaints he'd received from disgruntled listeners. They moaned if they got drenched when he'd not predicted rain, but if he predicted it and it didn't happen the organisers of events moaned they'd lost visitors.

"It's not my fault," Jeff continued. He showed her the reports from the station's parent company. "They don't give me much to go on."

That was true. The forecasts were for the entire region. By the time Jeff took out the parts that weren't relevant to their area and avoided any concrete assurances of particular weather which could lead to complaints there really wasn't anything left.

"Couldn't win whatever I did," he grumbled, reminding Gail of distant thunder. "Don't worry, lovey. Things'll be different for you."

She wondered why he was so sure of that. As she walked down the corridor she thought she got her answer. Sally the researcher said, "Here comes Ricky's little ray of sunshine."

Her breezily cheerful personality was an asset Jeff didn't possess. Gail spent the rest of the day beaming smiles at everyone, especially her employer.

"Really brighten the place up, you do," one of her new colleagues said. "I can see why Ricky hired you."

"Thank you!"

That evening there was a party for Jeff at the local pub. When Gail arrived she heard someone say, "Did you see her and Ricky making eyes at each other this afternoon?"

Did everyone think that? Gail knew if she hoped to be taken seriously she must scotch such rumours before they took hold. Although she'd been looking forward to getting to know Ricky better, she made a point of keeping away from him all evening.

Ricky offered her a lift home and it seemed to Gail that everyone was waiting to hear what she'd say. She hesitated. The east wind was bitterly cold. If she caught the bus she still had a fair walk in the dark and she couldn't afford a taxi.

"I go right past your road," Ricky said, making refusal difficult.

Determined not to give him the wrong impression, she spoke about work, telling him she'd rather do without the reports Jeff had been using and instead create her own forecasts from weather charts.

"Sure, if that's what you want."

"I do. Doing this job properly and professionally is very important to me."

"Which is one of the reasons I employed you." He spoke with warmth.

Oh, if only the other was that he really did think of her as his ray of sunshine. She shook her head to dislodge such an unprofessional thought. She was a qualified meteorologist not someone just there to look pretty and flirt with the producer, even if she'd rather like to.

For the rest of the journey, Gail talked rapidly about the latest forecasting techniques.

When Gail arrived early the following Monday there were no weather facts and charts for her to interpret. She had to go live on air and make it up. Her mind went blank and she simply repeated the stock phrases of Jeff's she'd used the previous week.

"Sorry, Gail," Sally said. "Ricky called and said not to get your report ready because you wouldn't need it."

Clearly he'd misunderstood what she'd said the night before. She explained what she needed and the researcher printed off the data. Gail's forecasts after that were detailed, specific to the area and accurate.

A week later Ricky called her into his office. He held up a sheaf of papers, reminding Gail of the complaints Jeff had shown her. She shivered. Perhaps her fears showed in her face because Ricky quickly said, "They're mostly praising your accuracy."

"Oh. Well, that's good."

He indicated for her to sit down. "Yes, very good. So you're settling in OK?"

"Yes. Thank you."

"And obviously doing a proper, professional job." He indicated the papers.

"Er, yes." She blushed as she remembered how sharp she'd been in an attempt to hide her feelings.

"Accuracy is important of course, but I think you might possibly be overdoing the professionalism."

"I'm sorry about that, Ricky. I..." She trailed off. She could hardly admit her feelings for him weren't professional at all.

"Our listeners tune in for entertainment as much as for information which, let's face it, they could easily get elsewhere. Could you be a bit more chatty do you think?"

"Chatty?" She spoke continuously throughout her whole broadcast.

"The few of these emails and letters that aren't praising you are saying they miss Jeff's easy to understand style. Not all our listeners know the difference between isobars and cumulative nimbies."

"Do you mean cumulonimbus?"

"Maybe. What does that do anyway?"

"It's a cloud formation... the one that looks like an explosion or as though someone's dropped an egg into sifted flour. It's often associated with storms because..."

"There you go then," he interrupted, ending the discussion.

During Gail's next broadcast a listener emailed in. Sally printed out his question and slipped it in front of Gail.

It read, 'Last week you mentioned a cumulo something. Do all clouds have different names?'

Gail read it out and said, "Yes they do, there's cirrus and mare's tail and mackerel." She repeated the description of a cumulonimbus and signed off.

The DJ motioned for her to stay. "I've heard of mackerel

skies, is that the same thing as mackerel cloud?" he asked, still on air.

"Yes, that's right."

"My gran used to talk about them as though they were a good thing."

"That's probably because they precede a weather front and signal a change of weather. Was your gran a keen gardener?"

"Yes! Very much so."

"Often when it's been dry for a while the mackerel sky is likely to soon be followed by rain so gardeners are often pleased to see them, but after a cold spell they can be pushed through by a warm front."

"That would explain it."

The DJ thanked her more enthusiastically than he ever had previously.

Gail kept the message Sally had printed for her. It was from 'Jack Frost'. Probably not his real name. Listeners often referred to themselves with nicknames such as 'Angie's Granddad' or 'Fifties Refugee'.

Ricky was waiting for her in the corridor. He nodded as she passed. "Much better."

Gail hoped he couldn't see the way her face glowed at his praise. Maybe technical terms, if properly explained, weren't really so unwelcome to the listening public?

She began describing one term per day and explaining how different information helped her to predict the weather. Soon listeners were ringing, writing and emailing in. Many were sympathetic about the difficulties of her job. Some asked questions for her to answer on air, such as, 'Is there any truth in red sky at night, shepherd's delight?' or 'Should we really worry about it raining on St Swithin's Day?' Jack Frost was the most frequent correspondent.

Gail soon learned to give the answers the day after she read the questions out, both to encourage people to tune in again and to give her time to research anything she didn't know. If only she could employ the same tactic to stop her saying the wrong thing when she talked to Ricky.

She had another question from Jack. 'They say when gorse is out of flower, kissing is out of fashion. Is there any weather you think is unsuitable for kissing?'

She read his question and answered, "I'm single, but in theory, no. A romantic summer sunset, cuddling up in front of a fire, sheltering together from the rain. With the right person it's all good."

Ricky called her into his office again. He offered her longer slots on some of the programmes and a corresponding rise in pay. He cut off her thanks with a brusque, "I have to give the listeners what they want."

But clearly not what he wanted personally.

The DJs and newsmen responded well to her on air but didn't chat to her much otherwise. Only Sally the researcher seemed friendly.

Gail asked her why the others kept their distance. "Is it because I'm a woman?"

"Sort of. Ricky's warned them off getting too pally with you. They're to treat you with professional courtesy but never go beyond that."

Oh dear. Not only had she alienated her charming boss, she'd ensured she made no friends inside the studio. At least the listeners loved her. She became a kind of weather agony aunt. Listeners asked such questions as, 'My daughter is getting married next June – should we risk an outdoor reception?' or 'What'll be the best night for our firework party' and 'How can I find someone to cuddle up to in bad weather?' That one was from Jack Frost.

She told him, on air, there were likely to be showers all week. If he were to carry an umbrella he could appear just in time to shelter his beloved.

That afternoon as she left the studio she was greeted by torrents of rain. Ricky appeared, grinning smugly, with his umbrella. "You should listen to our weather forecaster, she's really quite good."

"Yes, I should," she said through gritted teeth.

It wasn't until she'd driven off it occurred to her he'd provided shelter and complimented her work and she'd interpreted it as sarcasm. He was always friendly to her, she really shouldn't hold it against him that he stayed as professional as she'd claimed to want.

That worry was forgotten the next morning when a beautiful bouquet of unusual flowers arrived for her. It included a few sprays of gorse. Gail hardly needed to see the name scribbled after 'hope these bring a little sunshine into your life' on the attached card to know the flowers were from Jack Frost.

What a sweet thing for him to do. Thinking about it, Jack Frost had been the person who'd made her life bearable at work. He'd shown her how to improve her broadcasts, encouraged her as she improved and been the driving force behind her getting more air time and correspondingly better pay. She should thank him, but perhaps doing so on air wouldn't be professional. She didn't want to appear to be inviting gifts.

Gail asked the researcher for Jack's email address.

Sally looked uncomfortable. "We don't have it."

"Of course you do if he emailed in." Why was Sally being difficult? Did everyone in this place dislike her?

Never mind, she still had his first message in her desk. She retrieved it, but it didn't help. Usually when she was given the print-out of a listener's question or comment she got a screen shot, which included the sender's email and the time it was sent. With Jack Frost's she only had the actual message. They had all been like that, she suddenly realised; she'd easily spotted his in amongst the others. There must be a reason.

Gail returned to the office intending to demand an explanation. Sally wasn't there and the other girl was on the phone. Gail seized her chance. She jumped into Sally's seat and quickly scrolled through the station's emails. It didn't take long to find one with the subject 'message from Jack Frost'. As she'd expected that wasn't the sender's real name. What she hadn't guessed was that it was from Ricky.

"Oh no! You saw?" Sally said from behind her.

"I did. I don't understand though."

"He really likes you, but you made it so clear you wanted a professional relationship and nothing more, that he didn't dare say."

"I thought everyone here hated me."

"Of course not. The boys just kept their distance because they didn't want to seem to be competing with Ricky and the rest of us have been careful not to say too much."

Gail nodded. It made sense. "Don't worry, I won't tell him I found out from you."

"You're going to tell him?"

"Listen to my next broadcast... and try to get Ricky to listen too."

"No problem."

"Thanks, Sally."

During Gail's next weather forecast she said, "It's going to be very mild all week. Tonight though, I predict frost. Jack Frost that is, I'm hoping he'll join me for a drink at The Thunderbolt around seven and we can see if we melt each other's hearts."

23 Something Brewing

"Cup of tea, love?"

Joanne was up out of her chair and heading for the kitchen before she remembered she wasn't going to do that anymore; jump up the moment he mentioned tea like some dog obeying a command from its beloved master. She'd had it planned; she'd look up from the book she was reading, smile sweetly, say 'that'd be lovely thanks' and continue reading. Let him go fill the kettle for a change.

Thing was he'd caught her not actually doing anything. She'd just finished the book and added it to the others waiting to go back to the library and hadn't decided if she wanted to continue the embroidery she'd been working on or have another go at making the flower arrangement they'd been shown at the club last week. She could decide while making the tea she supposed, but that wasn't the point.

Yesterday she'd stood at the sink filling the kettle and got to wondering how many times she'd made tea for Linden. Once every morning before work, one when he got in and generally at least one more each evening. It'd been the same whether she'd been working or home with the kids and of course there were more at the weekends. Four times a day she'd guessed as an average and they'd been married forty-two years.

And that didn't take into account before they were married. Joanne made tea for him when he'd come to her parents' house and often when he'd taken her for a day out they'd made tea on a little gas stove. Or rather she always made it, that was the point. They'd used that same gas stove on their first holidays together as camping was all they could afford – and guess who got up first each morning and lit the darn thing to boil the kettle? All together it worked out as at least sixty-thousand mugs she'd calculated. Sixty-thousand and one; all those filled with tea, plus she felt a mug for doing it.

That's when she'd decided not to stand for it any more. Next time he wanted a mug of tea he could blessed well make it himself. She'd forgotten that morning and automatically made it while he was shaving.

She'd been a little annoyed with herself but then decided it would have been silly to wait thirsty until he came down, and petty to make hers but not his. Their morning routine was well established and she didn't really want to start changing it.

She'd waited until the mid-morning tea. But Linden had suggested they walk down to the market. He'd bought her an armful of flowers to practise with and they'd stopped in the coffee shop instead of having tea at home.

Their daughter had popped in at lunchtime to eat her sandwich with them and she'd made the tea for them all. It was odd, neither of the kids now expected tea on demand. When they visited they'd often make it and even when they'd been teenagers at home she'd had no trouble reminding them they knew where the kettle was if the wanted a drink. So why couldn't she do the same with Linden?

Joanne took her husband's favourite brand of tea bags from the cupboard and dropped one into each mug without really needing to look at what she was doing. Even when she didn't know where the kettle was any better than he did, because they were away on holiday, she'd made every cup. They always went self-catering. Linden didn't mind eating out and trying a few local dishes, but didn't think anywhere foreign could make a decent cup of tea.

Now the kids were grown and left and they had a little more money to spend they still went self-catering. Truth be told she enjoyed it, using the few phrases they'd learned of the language and buying food locally, even when they weren't always sure what they were getting, made her feel more immersed in the country than if she'd just ordered their old favourites in a restaurant. But it was her holiday too. After a day out in the blazing sun admiring tropical looking gardens and ornate buildings she'd have enjoyed sitting with her feet up in the cool apartment or maybe sitting out on the balcony enjoying the breeze in the evening instead of heading straight for the kitchen to boil water.

She'd thought of suggesting they went to China, or did she mean Japan? Whichever, they could see fields of tea bushes then go to one of those tea ceremonies and someone else would make tea for her. But then she'd had visions of Linden wanting her to dress like a geisha in future. Joanne stifled her giggle. She was annoyed with him and had every right to be. The spoon rattled as she stirred exactly half a spoonful of sugar into Linden's drink.

It wasn't just tea either. Linden liked something to nibble so she carried in the mugs then went back for biscuits. Well not anymore! She was putting her foot down. She'd made the tea now but he could jolly well get his own biscuit if he wanted one!

She carried the tea in and found him tidying a pot plant. She'd mentioned it was looking tatty when she'd looked up from finishing her book and spotted a few browning leaves and now he was carefully removing the old ones. He was better at that sort of thing than her. She'd have set to with shears and made it look worse if he hadn't got to it before her.

This time she allowed herself to grin. She had mentioned it looked sad in the hope he'd sort it out, but not because she'd expected him to jump at her command. A bit like him mentioning tea perhaps? Maybe he did it just hoping she'd put the kettle on and not because he thought she was his slave.

He had made tea before, she remembered now she thought about it. When she'd had morning sickness or been ill he'd made her a cup and coaxed her to drink it. When she'd been nursing the babies he'd often made tea for her. She remembered joking she felt like she was recycling it.

He'd also changed a lot of nappies while she'd brewed their drinks. In fact he almost always did do something rather than just sit and wait. He'd struggled with the tent on camping trips while she'd sorted out the tea things. He'd taken the kids for a long walk on holidays to calm them down after the flight whilst she'd found her way round a strange kitchen. Those holidays where she'd come in hot and bothered it was usually because they'd queued in the heat to see something she'd been interested in. He'd have been just as content to sit in a shady bar with a glass of something cold in the midday sun.

"Something up, love?" Linden reached to take the mugs from her.

She realised she'd been stood in the middle of the living room for some time watching, but not really seeing, him tidy the plant.

"Not at all." She gave him his tea. "Shall I fetch the custard creams or would you rather have a slice of Battenberg?"

"Oooh, cake I think, but I'll fetch it. Got to get rid of these leaves anyway."

Joanne sat down and sipped her tea.

24 Spring In The Trench

George crumpled the letter and let it drop. It contained hopes, happiness and courage, things he'd had once but which left him as easily as had the sheet of paper.

It wasn't just his wife's latest letter, though that was part of it. The first had been full of admiration for him in his smart uniform, pride that he was doing his duty, belief he'd be home soon, safe and well. It was full of love, plans for their future, happiness. That's how he'd been too. He'd actually been excited. Not, he'd told himself, the rash excitement of those first young men who'd volunteered. Those boys believed it would be over by Christmas and they'd be welcomed back as heroes after a thrilling, gallantly fought and gloriously won battle. It wasn't over by that Christmas, nor the next, nor '16. Even so when in June '17 George joined up he'd hoped he'd be back home for Christmas. Maybe it would never be over, not until there was no one left to kill or be killed. It wasn't gallant, it wasn't glorious and he didn't believe anyone could now win.

Still, excited he'd been at the start. He'd go abroad to places he'd read about and never thought to visit. Maybe the gardens of Versailles or one of Europe's ancient forests. The Black Forest perhaps as they drove the Boche back.

The training wasn't so bad. Tiring and dull, just a short preparation for what was to come. It'd be like drill practice and mock skirmishes without the boring bits. Digging trenches would be like gardening at home.

It wasn't. At home you don't go so deep but that's the least of it. You dig to create life. Colour, fragrance, beauty or maybe vegetables to keep you from being hungry. Trenches were like graves. Graves dug for men not yet dead. Then you sowed the ground with bullets and blood. Your blood, their blood, it didn't matter. Would he have gone if he'd known?

Yes. Yes, because he had no choice. Yes, because he wouldn't have believed. Couldn't have believed. How could anyone?

They'd sent him to a forest all right. What used to be one anyway. The limbs torn from the trees as they were from men. But George was prepared by then. He knew which grenade, which shell, had crippled a man, which had felled a pine. When the weapon was ours and the remains of a life theirs he was supposed to see victory. What was wrong with him that he couldn't rejoice at the sight?

But he was defending his country wasn't he? He was on the right side and keeping his wife safe. Safe from the Zeppelins? From fear? Hunger? No. But he was here now. He could fight and maybe die, or refuse and be shot. What did it matter? That's how he felt when he got the second letter. Well a handful of them all together, all the same.

The first written not long after he'd seen her last, but delayed in reaching him. The tone was positive and upbeat. George read between the lines. She was writing that way, not feeling it. Trying to be brave and strong for him. He knew because he wrote to her.

It was the last of them which hurt the most. The hope, the love, the optimism were all there for real. She was to have their baby and she'd seen in the paper that the war would be won soon. She'd have her hero husband back to help decorate the Christmas tree, if a tree could be got, and after the army presented his medals she'd present him with a child in the spring. He should start thinking of names.

George did. Alfred perhaps, after his father, if it were a boy. He smiled, or George after hers? For a moment he could see her answering smile when he suggested it. A ray of sun soon hidden by a dark cloud.

There was no spring and there were no more letters. Had she had the child? Had it lived? Did she?

Then out on patrol again. Why? There was nothing to protect. All was dead, black, destroyed. He stumbled into a man, or the man stumbled into him. They fell together, too tired to get up. Too tired for a long time even to see their uniforms weren't the same. He was the enemy. Evil. Hated. But George was too tired to see much more than a man, tired as he was. Too tired even to wish for the strength to kill him. George slept and when he woke was alone. Alone holding a twig. No olive branch but a beech, with soft young leaves. He told no one for he couldn't quite understand what had happened. What it meant.

Now he knew spring had come he saw it everywhere. The blasted, twisted trees were launching a counter attack. Exploding life, freshness and innocence back into the world. The earth too was pushing up hopeful shoots through the black.

Another letter, recent. Not in his wife's hand. The child was a girl. 'Mother and baby doing well. No name yet, they're waiting for you to come home.' How long would they have to wait? Too long perhaps.

The letter had been written on his daughter's birthday. His wife would have been tired. George understood tiredness. Hers might pass. The child might thrive. She'd learn to smile and crawl and stand and speak. She'd know nothing of him. Care nothing for him.

Months passed. He heard nothing more from home. Other,

official messages came. In late autumn they learned there was going to be an end. When the eleventh hour of the eleventh day of the eleventh month passed, war would be over. Could that be true? Everyone said it was, but could it really be true? Was war not all there was now? George remembered the twig with its shoots of green and he too believed.

Then a letter, much delayed, from his wife. Paeony, that was his daughter's name. 'Sorry, George that I didn't wait, but she needed a name. I was tired after the birth and I missed you, my love. Then I looked out and saw the paeony in bloom, the pink one you planted on our first anniversary. I know you've not seen either the bloom or our beautiful daughter, but you will. I know you will.'

George closed his eyes and saw them. Not Paeony's features, not the petals now faded, but as he'd seen spring in the forest. And he loved them. He loved his wife and he loved his daughter. He wouldn't be there for a while yet, but he would be there and as his daughter grew, she'd learn to love him as he loved her.

George crumpled the letter and held it against his heart. It was joy and hope and love. Those things flooded through him as real and certain as the sheet of paper pressed to his chest.

Thank you for reading this book. I hope you enjoyed it. If you did, I'd really appreciate it if you could leave a short review on Amazon and/or Goodreads.

To learn more about my writing life, hear about new releases and get a free short story, sign up to my newsletter – https://mailchi.mp/677f65e1ee8f/sign-up or you can find the link on my website patsycollins.uk

More books by Patsy Collins

Novels –

Firestarter
Escape To The Country
A Year And A Day
Paint Me A Picture
Leave Nothing But Footprints
Acting Like A Killer

Non-fiction –

From Story Idea To Reader
(co-written with Rosemary J. Kind)

A Year Of Ideas:
365 sets of writing prompts and exercises

Short story collections –

Up The Garden Path
Through The Garden Gate
In The Garden Air
No Family Secrets
Can't Choose Your Family
Keep It In The Family
Family Feeling
Happy Families
All That Love Stuff
With Love And Kisses
Lots Of Love
Love Is The Answer
Slightly Spooky Stories I
Slightly Spooky Stories II
Slightly Spooky Stories III
Slightly Spooky Stories IV
Just A Job
Perfect Timing
A Way With Words
Dressed To Impress
Coffee & Cake
Criminal Intent
Not A Drop To Drink